Cursed with a poor sense of direction and a propensity to read, **Annie Claydon** spent much of her childhood lost in books. A degree in English Literature followed by a career in computing didn't lead directly to her perfect job—writing romance for Mills & Boon—but she has no regrets in taking the scenic route. She lives in London: a city where getting lost can be a joy.

Also by Annie Claydon

Resisting Her English Doc
Festive Fling with the Single Dad
Best Friend to Royal Bride
Winning the Surgeon's Heart
A Rival to Steal Her Heart
Healing the Vet's Heart
The Best Man and the Bridesmaid

London Heroes miniseries

Falling for Her Italian Billionaire
Second Chance with the Single Mum

Discover more at millsandboon.co.uk.

GREEK ISLAND FLING TO FOREVER

ANNIE CLAYDON

MILLS & BOON

First published in Great Britain 2021
by Mills & Boon, an imprint of HarperCollins*Publishers* Ltd,
1 London Bridge Street, London, SE1 9GF

www.harpercollins.co.uk

HarperCollins*Publishers*
1st Floor, Watermarque Building,
Ringsend Road, Dublin 4, Ireland

Large Print edition 2021

Greek Island Fling to Forever © 2021 Annie Claydon

ISBN: 978-0-263-28793-6

08/21

MIX
Paper from
responsible sources
FSC® C007454

This book is produced from independently certified
FSC™ paper to ensure responsible forest management.
For more information visit www.harpercollins.co.uk/green.

Printed and bound in Great Britain
by CPI Group (UK) Ltd, Croydon, CR0 4YY

CHAPTER ONE

THE DAY THAT had changed her life had been bright and clear, bathed in sunshine, and every detail was still sharp in Arianna's dreams. She was six years old and had insisted on wearing her new white *broderie anglaise* dress for the journey to the Petrakis family's holiday home on the tiny Greek island of Ilaria.

Her father had frowned when he heard the news that their own launch was out of action, and her mother had smiled as if it was of no consequence and said they'd take the ferry. It had been a new experience for Arianna and her older brother, Xander, waiting with the jostling crowd of other passengers to board, and then finding a place on deck where her mother could sit.

Even her father had loosened up a bit, opening the collar of his shirt and gesturing to their bodyguard to take a family photograph.

Then he'd acceded to Xander's excited demands and agreed to take him on a tour of the large, exciting craft. Xander had turned, waving to her as they'd walked away.

Her mother had been wearing a wide-brimmed hat and a red and white fitted sundress, so different from the faded colours she wore now. She'd perched on a slatted wooden bench and started to talk to the other mothers, telling Arianna that she could go and play if she wanted, as long as she stayed close.

The ferry had slowly manoeuvred out of the busy dock, speeding up a little as it entered the blue waters of the Mediterranean. Arianna had wished they could take this route every time, and when Ilaria had begun to loom on the horizon she'd wanted the island to stay away for a while longer, so that they could spend a little more time on the ferry.

Then... Then a juddering, crashing sound. The world tipped suddenly and she fell, grazing her knees on the wooden deck. She heard her mother screaming her name, but she was sliding, falling. Somehow, the water seemed to rear up and grab her, pulling her down.

She couldn't breathe... And then something…someone…was there. Grabbing her flailing arms and holding her tight. Their heads broke the surface, and muffled sounds turned into a chaos of shouting and screaming. She could breathe enough to choke and cry, and when she opened her eyes, blinking against the sting of the salt, she saw an older boy with a shock of blond hair, wet and plastered around his face.

He said something to her, but she didn't understand the words. She understood safety, though, and when he wound her arms around his neck she hung on tight. They bobbed together in the water, and then the boy started to swim, labouring hard while Arianna clung onto his back.

She didn't dare look behind her. Maybe if she had, she would have caught one last glimpse of Xander. But ahead there were small boats, leaving the tiny port of Ilaria and making their way towards them.

Arianna was sobbing now, and the boy stopped swimming. More words that she didn't understand, but which made her feel safe again. The water was pulling them back, towards the sinking ferry, and he began to strike out again, towards the rescue boats. She closed her eyes, reciting the prayer that her mother always said with her before she lay down to sleep.

Then she felt strong hands around her and she was lifted out of the water. One of the boats had reached them, and the boy had pushed her up into the arms of its occupants. A man held her tight as she reached back for the boy, but a wave carried him away. She started to scream and cry as his blond head disappeared amongst the waves and the scattered mass of people in the sea.

And then... The memories lost their clarity. She remembered her mother crying and her father hugging her until she could hardly breathe, when they found her, wrapped in a blanket and sitting amongst a group of survivors in the taverna, which had opened its doors to provide shelter and warm drinks. And she remembered her father, kissing her mother and running back down to the boats that were ferrying people back to the shore.

He'd been gone a long time, but her mother had refused to move, holding Arianna tight as they both shivered in the warm breeze. When he finally *had* returned, he was alone. Her mother had taken one look at his face and screamed in anguish…

Arianna sat bolt upright in her bed, feeling the cold sweat beading her forehead. Returning to Ilaria, to establish a medical practice here, had left little time for anything other than work. Now that the pressure was off during the day her dreams at night had become more frequent and much more vivid. Breathing deeply to steady her racing heart, Arianna told herself it wasn't necessarily a bad thing and that perhaps she needed to get the trauma of that day, twenty-five years ago, out of her system. And it was one more precious chance to see Xander again, along with the blond-haired boy who had carried her to safety and then disappeared amongst the waves.

The boy hadn't drowned. Later, when she was older, she'd traced everyone who had died that day and there was no one matching his description on the list. He'd just disappeared in the melee of survivors. He was out there somewhere, grown up now, and Arianna wondered if he ever thought of her.

* * *

It was a bright, warm day. Ben Marsh stepped off the ferry, pulling the map of Ilaria's harbour town from his pocket and looking around to get his bearings.

He'd wondered if he might remember this place when he saw it; he'd thought about it often enough over the years. But he didn't. There was nothing familiar about the ferry terminus, but it was a new building, obviously constructed since he'd last been here, twenty-five years ago. Ben made a beeline for the tourist information booth and a smiling woman welcomed him to the island and marked the position of the health centre on his map for him.

He walked to the main harbour, stopping to scan the small boats moored there. None of them were familiar either, although in truth he'd been too intent on scanning the horizon to look for other survivors to remember much about the craft whose crew had finally pulled him out of the sea. And the people? The frightened little girl who had clung to his back as he'd swum away from the sinking ferry would be beyond recognition now. She could be any one of the young women who passed him in the street, and Ben told himself that searching their faces for any shred of recognition was a waste of time.

But he knew her name. Arianna Petrakis. It had been six months since he'd stumbled on an old newspaper account that had answered the questions he'd wondered about for so long, and since then the name had seemed to resound in his head.

Icy fingers skittered from his neck, down his spine, and he shivered in the sunshine. What if she didn't want to see him? The answer to that was easy; he'd take the next ferry off the island and go. What if she *did* want to see him? How could he explain that the day the ferry had sunk had shaped his life? Could he even begin to say that now he had the strangest feeling that he needed Arianna to rescue him?

Ben shook off the questions, knowing he had no answer to them. Jumping into the water to save Arianna had been the first defining moment of change in his life. The second had been crushingly different. He'd made a solemn vow to love and cherish, and then not been there when his wife had needed him. Emma was gone now, and Ben couldn't turn back the clock and save her.

But he hadn't thought twice when he'd seen the little girl in the white dress sliding across the deck of the ferry and falling into the water. He'd jumped. And now he needed to do that again, to just follow his instincts and jump.

After a steep climb up the hill, away from the harbour, he found the health centre. He shouldn't have worried whether he'd recognise it—the stone wall that bordered the road had a large notice in six different languages, and when he opened the gate he saw a modern building nestled behind a small garden that was a riot of colour and scent. Automatic doors swished open and he found himself in a large reception area, welcoming and cool after the sticky heat. A woman was watering a large plant that stood in one corner and turned to greet him.

Ben's heart jumped. But no, it couldn't be her. Dark curls could be dyed and straightened into the woman's smart, honey-blonde style, but if he had to guess her age he would have settled at late thirties. Older than Arianna would be. And surely he would recognise Arianna if he came face to face with her?

'*Yassas...*'

The woman's smile indicated that she appreciated him making the effort to greet her in Greek, but it was unnecessary. 'Hello. My name is Corinna. How may I help you?'

'I'm looking for Dr Petrakis.'

'You are sick?' Corinna looked him up and down.

'No... My name's Ben Marsh. Dr Ben Marsh.' Maybe the *Dr* part would convince her that he was here on business of some kind, and she wouldn't enquire any further.

Corinna nodded, shrugging slightly. 'Take a seat, please. Dr Petrakis will be back in five minutes.'

Ben sat down, looking around him. Light and spacey, cool white walls and earth tones for the furniture. Someone had thought through this area carefully, to provide a welcoming and relaxing area, but his heart was pumping hard. He took his phone from his pocket, opening up the app for the British papers and hoping that Corinna would take this as a signal not to engage him in any further conversation.

She finished watering the plants and then returned to her seat, concentrating her attention on the computer screen in front of her. The doors swished open but it was only a courier, bringing a parcel. After fifteen minutes, Corinna spoke again.

'I'm sure she will be here soon. Would you like me to call her?'

'No, please don't. I'm happy to wait until she returns.'

'You would like a drink...?'

The doors swished open again and Ben's heart jumped. When his head snapped instinctively towards the entrance, he saw a young woman and a dark-haired man supporting a blonde-haired girl between them. The man was clearly a passer-by who had stopped to help, calling Corinna by name and speaking in Greek to her, then turning to leave as she began to rap out orders.

'She is having an asthma attack. Sit her down. Dr Marsh, as you are here you must help her. I will call Dr Petrakis...' A flip of her finger towards Ben, and then Corinna picked up the phone.

He wasn't licensed to practise in Greece, but that was a moot point at the moment. The blonde-haired girl was clearly in distress and this was an emergency. Ben hurried over to the girls, guiding them over to the seats.

'Does she have an inhaler?'

'Yes, but she forgot it. It's back at our hotel…' The girl's companion's eyes were wide with panic.

'Okay. That's okay.' It wasn't, but what he needed to do now was to calm both girls. 'What's her name?'

'Helen…'

Ben turned to Helen, taking her gently by the shoulders. 'Helen, I'm Ben and I'm a doctor. Look at me…'

Helen's frightened gaze met his. Ben smiled reassuringly.

'I want you to try to calm down. Try to breathe more slowly for me, yes?'

Helen nodded. The panic and the rush to the health centre hadn't done her a great deal of good, and now that she was sitting down she seemed a little better. Helen turned as her friend started to cry and Ben put one finger on the side of her face, guiding her gaze back onto him.

'Don't worry about anyone else. Just look at me. Try to breathe with me.'

Corinna had finished her call. 'Dr Petrakis will be here in five minutes. She will bring the inhaler from the chemist.'

Ben nodded. 'Thanks. Perhaps you could look after this young lady?' He indicated Helen's friend and Corinna jumped to her feet, guiding the girl away from them and to a spare seat behind her desk.

'What colour is your inhaler, Helen?' Ben smiled again at her. 'Blue?'

A nod.

'Good. Albuterol?' Ben hadn't yet come across anyone with asthma who didn't know exactly what drug they needed, and he hoped this wouldn't be a first.

Another nod. Helen was calming now and her breathing was slower, but she was still having to work too hard to get the oxygen her body needed.

'Okay, that's great.' Ben turned to Corinna, who already had her phone in her hand, the other arm tightly around the other girl's shoulders. 'Will you tell Dr Petrakis…?'

'Albuterol. I heard…' Corinna shot him a stern look, clearly outraged at any implication that she didn't have everything under control, and Ben turned back to Helen again.

'You're doing really well, Helen.' Hopefully the promised five minutes before Arianna Petrakis got here from the pharmacy wouldn't be as long as the five minutes he'd been asked to wait.

'Don't…let me…' Helen was struggling to speak.

Die. Don't let her die. The last few years had shown Ben that he was powerless in the face of life and death, but Helen didn't need to know that.

'I'm not going to let you do anything. Apart from breathe. That's okay with you?'

This time Helen returned his smile, nodding.

'Will you bring her through to surgery?' Corinna had finished relaying the message and put her phone back down on her desk.

'Yes, that would be a good idea.' Anything

to keep Helen quiet and away from any hub-bub in the main reception area.

Corinna nodded, turning to Helen's friend and telling her firmly not to move. Then she beckoned to Ben.

Helen wasn't ready to walk yet. Ben grinned at her. 'Let's do this the easy way, shall we? Hold onto me.'

He bent, picking Helen up. He could feel her breathing against his chest, as she lay in his arms, and he followed Corinna to a modern, well equipped surgery, putting Helen down on the examination couch and operating the backrest so that she was sitting up.

'Thanks…' Helen seemed to be breathing a little more easily now.

'That's okay. I get extra points on the emergency doctor scale for carrying someone, you know. I'm just glad you aren't too heavy.'

Helen smiled, even though the joke wasn't really so much of a joke. Ben had just done his job, what he needed to do to keep Helen quiet and safe. But somehow, that lost feeling of being able to make a difference had filtered back into the equation. Maybe because of Helen, but more likely because Arianna

Petrakis was just five minutes away now, and she'd known him when he *could* make a difference.

Ben saw a light blanket draped across the bottom of the couch and pulled it up over Helen's legs. She was beginning to recover now, although the smallest thing could leave her struggling for breath again. The door to the surgery opened quietly and Ben turned.

Arianna. He'd know her anywhere. Dark curls, cut to frame her face. Liquid brown eyes, and flawless olive skin. There was something about the way she carried herself that reminded him of the bravery of the little girl who had clung so tightly to him, and... there was no getting away from it...she was beautiful.

'Hi, I'm Dr Petrakis.' Her manner was perfect, assured and relaxed, even though the pink in her cheeks suggested that she might have been running to get here. 'You're Helen?'

Helen nodded, and Arianna put a large paper pharmacy bag onto her desk. 'I've got a selection of inhalers, but Dr Marsh says that the blue one with Albuterol is the one you usually have.'

'Yes, that's right.' Helen seemed much better now, and managed to get three words out without gasping for breath.

'That's good; I have the one you need.' Arianna reached for the bag, taking a box out and reading the Greek lettering on the side, before opening it and taking out the inhaler.

Her English was flawless, and spoken with a slight London accent, the kind you didn't get from just learning the language. The thought that maybe she'd lived in Ben's home town and he'd never known how close she was took Ben's breath away, and then Arianna turned her gaze onto him.

'Thank you, Dr Marsh.' He thought he saw some spark of recognition, but maybe it was just in his imagination. 'I'll examine Helen now. Corinna will make you some coffee, if you still want to wait?'

Yes, of course… He was a tourist who'd just helped out in an emergency, and it was time for him to leave.

'Thanks. I'll wait.' He turned to Helen with a smile. 'You're looking much better now.'

Helen gave him a smile and a thumbs up, and Ben returned the gesture before walking back out into the reception area. He didn't really want coffee, but Corinna insisted on making him some, putting a selection of biscuits on a plate next to his cup. He sipped his drink as he waited, before Arianna appeared again.

'Claire, you can go and see Helen now.' She spoke to Helen's friend, who'd been sitting miserably in the corner, despite all of Corinna's attempts to cheer her up. 'She's much better, but she needs to rest a little. Andreas, our paramedic, has just arrived and he's sitting with her. Be calm and quiet, yes?'

Claire nodded. 'I'm sorry...'

Arianna batted the apology away with a flick of her hand. 'It's frightening to see someone taken ill like that, isn't it? Now that she's here, we can look after her and she'll be fine. What she needs right now is to see you smiling.'

Arianna was being kind. The hurried rush through the streets to the health centre couldn't have done Helen any good; it would have been better to keep her sitting down and get help to come to her. Maybe she'd explain that at some point, but Ben had little doubt that her firm, gentle way would make it sound like a bit of advice for the future rather than a condemnation.

Claire wiped away her tears and tried out a smile, and Arianna gave her an approving nod. Corinna took Claire's hand, leading her towards the surgery, and then Ben's heart started to beat a little faster as Arianna turned to walk across the reception area towards him.

CHAPTER TWO

MAYBE IT WAS the last dregs of her dream.
It had been so clear, and Arianna had struggled to break free of it as she'd showered and
made breakfast this morning. But when she'd
walked into her surgery, the handsome English doctor had made her catch her breath.
There was something so familiar about him.

She'd managed to quell the feeling as she
examined and treated Helen, but now that
Andreas was back from his afternoon visits
and would sit with Helen while she recov-
ered it had started to nag at her again. And
when she caught sight of Dr Marsh again, sitting in the waiting room, she was even more
convinced she knew him. From a day years
ago, when a blond-haired, blue-eyed boy had
saved her from the sea.

It was impossible. That kind of coincidence
just didn't happen, even if it had occupied her
daydreams for much of her teens. And her

dreams as an adult. Dr Ben Marsh was probably here for…something else. Some*one* else.

He got to his feet as she approached him, all hard lines and male beauty. Maybe that was why he seemed so familiar. He was definitely the kind of man that any woman would *want* to know.

'Dr Petrakis…'

'Arianna, please. Since we've already put you to work. You're on holiday here?' His casual trousers and shirt didn't indicate that he was here on business.

'I came to Ilaria to see you.'

Okay. Maybe she *did* know him from somewhere. But that still didn't mean Ben Marsh was the man a part of her hoped he was. Although it really shouldn't be necessary to search her memory for someone as strikingly attractive as Ben. Maybe Arianna's resolution to have nothing more to do with any man who looked capable of sweeping her off her feet had worked a little too well.

'I'm sorry… Have we met before?'

'If you're the Arianna Petrakis I think you are, then yes. It was a long time ago, though…'

He was obviously wary, clearly unwilling to spring anything on her, but now Arianna wondered if her instincts had been right.

'You were on the ferry? The one that sank just outside the harbour?' Her heart was pounding in her chest, as if her life depended on his answer.

'Yes. You were there too, wearing a white dress.'

'Broderie anglaise?' The detail seemed suddenly important.

'I think so. It had little embroidered holes—is that what they call it?'

'Yes. You dived in when I fell overboard.'

He smiled suddenly. *'Dived* makes it sound a lot more expert than it actually was. I saw you sliding across the deck and when you fell into the water I jumped in after you.'

'I was drowning…' The memory made her catch her breath. 'You pulled me up.'

'I don't know how I found you. Somehow I did.' He took a step forward, holding out his hand to shake hers. Arianna took it, winding her fingers tightly around his.

Once she did, she couldn't let go. Arianna willed her fingers to loosen around his but they wouldn't respond. She was clinging to him as tightly as she had that day in the water.

Then, she'd been blinded by tears and panic, and the men in the boat had been forced to prise her arms from around his neck. Things were different now. Ben was no longer a skinny youth, and Arianna was old enough to recognise that he now had that indefinable *something* that rendered a man attractive rather than just handsome.

'You still have a tight grip.' He smiled suddenly.

'Uh…sorry.' Still she couldn't let him go.

'Don't be. I needed you to hold on while I swam.'

'Is that what you said to me?' One last detail clicked into place.

'Yes. You didn't understand?'

'No. I didn't speak English then…'

If twenty-five years of longing to see him had taught Arianna anything, it had taught her restraint. She finally released his hand, feeling a chill of regret as she did so.

'We can't talk here. Can I take you for coffee somewhere?'

He shook his head. 'I should come back to-morrow. You have things to do here.'

The thought of him walking away now, of having to wait for a whole day before she could talk to him was impossible.

'It's all right. I start work early and I should be finishing around now anyway. Andreas covers at the clinic in the afternoons and early evenings, so he'll be here with Helen for a few hours and he'll give me a call if he needs me. If she's not well enough to go back to her hotel tonight, we have a three-bed ward here and I can come back and stay the night...'

She was babbling. It would have been enough to say that she had a few hours free and plenty of time for coffee. Maybe throw in a few words about what a pleasure it was to see him after all this time...

'How about this? The last ferry is at nine, and if Helen's well enough then I can go with her and Claire and make sure that they get back to their hotel. In the meantime, I'd like it very much if we could go for coffee.'

'That would be... Do you mind?'

'As long as you're willing to discharge

Helen medically, so that I'm just a concerned member of the public travelling with her.' He grinned.

'Of course. I'll go and get my bag.' Arianna flew out of the waiting room, grudging every moment that it took for her to check carefully on Helen and tell Andreas that she'd be down at the harbour if he needed her. It seemed as if she'd been waiting for this meeting all her life, and she didn't want to waste a second of it.

It felt like a dream. Finally Ben had found the girl who'd changed his life, and it felt as if he'd spent every day with her since their first meeting. In some ways he had. He'd got on with his life, but there hadn't been many days when a brief thought of her hadn't flashed through his mind.

Numbly, he followed her out of the health centre and back down the hill towards the harbour. They walked in silence. This was too big a thing for small talk, and Ben wasn't sure where to start with the things that really mattered.

'Is here all right?' She pointed to a small

taverna, which looked out over the harbour, with seats outside that were shaded from the late afternoon sun.

'It looks great.' Anywhere would be fine. Ben had the feeling that Arianna would shine in the darkest of dungeons, and that her dress would still shimmer around her legs in the same way.

She chose a table to one side of the bustle of the main seating area, and sat down. A waiter appeared, greeting Arianna by name, and she asked Ben what he'd like and then ordered in Greek.

'I'm glad you came, Ben. It's good to see you.' Now that they were finally able to talk, she seemed a little unsure of herself.

'I wasn't sure if you would be.' He felt strong suddenly. As if once more he should protect her from whatever she was feeling.

'What makes you say that?'

'I read… What led me to you was a news article. It said that your brother had been on the ferry, and that he drowned.'

'Yes. That's right.' Arianna's frank gaze found his. 'I would have drowned too, if it hadn't been for you.'

Ben shrugged. 'If my coming here is an unwelcome reminder of that day, then… I'd like you to tell me.'

'You think I could ever forget about it?' Arianna raised one eyebrow.

'No. I can't forget and… I had to come…'

She pursed her lips in thought. The waiter reappeared, unloading a tray of drinks and snacks and disappearing just as abruptly. Arianna reached for her coffee, taking a sip.

'I've never forgotten you, and I've always wondered what became of you. And now I know your name at last.' She gave him a smile that made Ben's heart lurch.

'And I've found out that *broderie anglaise* is the correct description for that dress of yours.'

She laughed suddenly. 'So we've both got some answers. I've always wondered about what happened to you after you lifted me into that boat. Tell me what you've been doing all my life.'

It was tempting to tell Arianna that he'd been waiting for *her.* That wasn't entirely true. Ben had done many other things, but wondering about the little girl in the white dress had probably been his most long-term preoccupation. And, lately, jumping into the water after her had seemed to be one of the few things he'd done exactly right.

Was he about to put all of that at risk? Turn the perfect memory into something vulnerable, which could be destroyed by the present? But when he looked at Arianna he couldn't believe that she would destroy anything.

'Right from the beginning?' He took a gulp of his coffee, feeling the strong taste hit the back of his throat.

'Yes. How did you get back to the shore—did you swim all the way?'

'I was a pretty strong swimmer and I reckoned I could make it. But I was very glad when someone saw me and a boat came to pick me up. It was a bit different from swimming in the pool at home. So was attempting to rescue someone.'

'I'll bet.' Arianna leaned back in her chair. 'Those dummies they use in the pool don't wriggle quite as much as I remember doing.'

'They don't hang on as tight as you did either. You were very brave.'

She smiled suddenly, and Ben wondered

if anyone had ever told her that. 'You were the only thing I had to hang onto. I owe you my life.'

Something warm and proud bloomed in Ben's chest. That feeling had changed *his* life and guided him through all of his darkest days. He owed Arianna his life as well, but didn't quite know how to say it.

'Well…' He decided to stick to the bare facts of the matter. 'The boat picked up a few more people and then took us all back to the harbour. I managed to find my parents and my brother and sister, and got a real telling-off from my dad for running off.'

'You didn't tell him that you'd saved someone?'

Ben shook his head. 'No. I felt… It felt so good that… I wanted that feeling all for myself so I kept it a secret.'

'Which is why I could never find any reference to you when I looked back on the news coverage. I knew that you'd survived, though, because you weren't amongst the list of casualties.' Arianna smiled. 'Another mystery solved.'

The thought gave a whole new meaning to his memories. 'You looked for me?'

'Of course I did. You were my superhero, appearing out of nowhere to save me and then disappearing again. Whatever makes you think I wouldn't look?'

He wasn't the hero that Arianna thought he was. He was flawed, capable of the best and the worst, and pretty much everything in between. Maybe this was why he'd decided to come, after all the heart-searching and uncertainty. He wanted to get back in touch with what he *could* do. It was a way of believing in himself again.

He began to tell the rest of his story. How the hotel where they'd been staying had heard that the ferry had sunk, and sent out a boat to bring them back to the mainland. How the holiday had ended and he'd gone back to England. Back to school, and then onto medical school.

'What made you want to be a doctor?' Arianna shot him a quizzical look.

'The same as anyone, I suppose. I wanted to make a difference.'

'Because you already knew that you could?'

'That day on the ferry… I've never forgotten how it felt. When I was younger, I thought my whole life could be like that.' Ben quirked the corners of his mouth down, knowing how naïve that teenage notion was now. He hadn't really meant to discuss this with Arianna.

'It changed you, then. You wanted to feel that way again.'

'Yes, it did. It meant a lot to me.'

It was as close as Ben could get to telling Arianna how much he needed her now. Her gaze was steady on his face and perhaps she understood a little of what he hadn't said, as well as that which he had.

'And after medical school?'

That all seemed easier to say, now. 'I did most of the usual things. Got a job, worked hard. Fell in love and got married. We bought a house and then our son, Jonas, came along, and redefined the meaning of tired.'

'I've heard they do that. Are your wife and son here in Greece? I'd love to meet them.'

'Jonas is here. We're staying at a hotel on the mainland with my sister and her family. My wife, Emma, died in a car accident four years ago, when Jonas was a year old.' The words had lost their sting now. Time was a healer, which had softened the pain of grief. The pain of guilt was a different matter, and Ben never talked about that.

Arianna's hand flew to her mouth. 'Oh. I'm so sorry, Ben.'

'It's…' He shrugged. 'It's not okay, but I live with it. Maybe you feel the same about your brother?'

She thought for a moment. 'I never quite accepted that I was the one who survived.'

That was how Ben felt too, and he had good reason. It had been his fault that Emma was alone in the car with Jonas, and her quick and selfless reactions had meant their son had escaped the crash unharmed. No amount of guilt and regret was going to change that now, and no amount of sharing would either.

Arianna's eyes glistened in the setting sun, and Ben fancied that he saw tears. There was something that Arianna wasn't saying, but he wouldn't press her. There were things he wasn't saying as well.

'Being the one that's left behind is difficult, isn't it?'

She nodded. 'How do you deal with it?'

He didn't. That wasn't for anyone to hear either.

'Let's just say that it took the edge off my belief in being able to change the world. The first year was very hard. The following one was better and then…one evening about six months ago, after I'd put Jonas to bed, I was searching the internet for some ideas on child-friendly holiday destinations. Ilaria came up and it reminded me of you. I couldn't resist searching one more time for information about the passengers on the ferry that day, and found an old newspaper article. I didn't understand it, it was written in Greek, but there was a picture of you and your family. Once I knew your name, I had to find you.'

'And you turned up and saved the day for Helen. As soon as she *could* talk, she told me how kind you'd been to her.'

Ben shook his head. 'I don't believe in turning up and saving the day any more.'

He had, once. But he'd neither turned up nor saved the day for Emma. It had been a salutary lesson.

She leaned forward, taking a matchbook from the holder on the table and lifting the glass shade from the candle that stood next to it. The match flared, and in the candle-light Ben thought he saw hope reflected in her eyes.

'Maybe you should. Ilaria's taught me a few things since I've been here. It might have some things to teach you too.'

Maybe. Ben wouldn't bet on it, but he wouldn't have bet on Arianna having given him a second thought over the years either. Perhaps this was a place where anything was possible.

He searched her face, looking carefully for any clue that she was speaking out of kindness. But even though he'd burst into her life with no warning, reminding her of many things that she'd probably rather forget, he could see no hint of regret. It empowered him to ask, 'Will you tell me what you've been doing with the last twenty-five years?'

CHAPTER THREE

IT WAS THE obvious question. Arianna had asked it of Ben and he'd answered. Now it was her turn, and it felt much more challenging than sitting listening to him.

'You've read the papers. You know who my father is. You probably know all you need to know.'

Who her father was. The death of her brother. The fact that she'd been saved and Xander hadn't. If anyone wanted to sum her up in three short sentences, then they covered pretty much everything.

'Your father is Ioannis Petrakis.' He said the name with an English inflection which made it sound unfamiliar to Arianna. 'That's part of the reason I succeeded in finding you; he's an important man and the newspapers report on what he does. With pictures.'

Arianna turned the corners of her mouth down. The thought that he was only here because of her father's wealth and position left a sour taste in her mouth. Ben was the one thing she'd kept entirely for herself over all these years, and suddenly even that seemed to be slipping away.

'Then you'll know that I was a spoiled rich kid.'

He shrugged. 'I know that your father's a rich man, but… I don't know you well enough to say whether or not you were spoiled. In my experience, when kids are wet through and terrified they're just kids.'

'We were only on the ferry because my father's launch had engine trouble. I loved it; it was so colourful and loud. After Xander died, I didn't get much of a chance to do anything that was colourful or loud. My father wouldn't allow it.'

He nodded slowly. 'It's a temptation, for any parent. My son's beginning to realise that there's a world out there and he wants to start exploring it. When Emma died I just wanted to lock him away and keep him safe.'

If Arianna could have seen Ben's anguished look mirrored on her father's face then maybe she would have understood a little better. But she never had…

'My father…he *did* lock us away. It suffocated my mother, and she sued for divorce when I was fourteen.'

'It's one of the hardest things that anyone can ever face. The death of a child.'

He understood. He'd struggled with his own loss. Her father hadn't seemed to struggle, he'd just ruled his family with a rod of iron, but Arianna felt that she could understand that a little better now.

'There was never really any room for anything else but grief with my parents. I tried to be a good child and not make things worse for them, but I could never really measure up to the son they'd lost.'

Ben shifted in his chair, clearly thinking the matter over. She liked that. He thought about things, tempering his gut reactions with his head and his heart.

'So you decided to measure yourself by what you wanted, instead?'

'Yes. I couldn't make a difference on the day my brother died, but I can make one now. My father threatened to cut me off when I applied to medical school in Athens but he just reduced my allowance to more than I ever needed.'

'But you've spent time in London.' Arianna shot him a questioning look and he smiled. 'Your accent. No one's second language is *that* good unless they've lived in a place.'

'We came to live in London when I was eleven. My parents' last-ditch attempt to get away from their grief and save their marriage. I went to school in Regent's Park.'

His lips curved suddenly into an incredulous smile that made her shiver. 'You had a straw boater as part of your uniform in the summer? With a blue ribbon?'

'Yes, the blue matched our blazers and dresses…' Arianna had hated the old-fashioned uniform of the high-class school for young ladies that seemed as if it was taken straight out of the nineteen-seventies.

'I was at medical school nearby. Whenever we got a break during the afternoons we'd go and sit in the park.'

They both smiled at the same time, the idea hanging in the air between them. Maybe he'd seen her. Maybe she'd seen him, one of the young men by the lake who'd seemed so free in comparison to her own closeted existence. If fate hadn't managed to engineer a meeting between them, it hadn't been through any lack of effort.

They'd been in the same places, seeing the same things. If Arianna had known that, maybe her teens would have felt a little less lonely. Or maybe not. Somehow it felt as if Ben had always been there. He already felt like an old friend, someone she hadn't been in touch with for a while, but still close enough to pick up a conversation where they'd left it last.

'I came back to London after I graduated from medical school. I applied for a newly qualified doctors exchange programme and worked at a medical centre near Charing Cross.'

He nodded. 'My practice is near there.'

Another chance to pass in the street. To go to the same restaurants and bars. It was tempting to reel off a list of places and wonder if he knew them too, but the fact that they'd breathed the same air seemed enough at the moment, because now they *had* met.

'You must like London then?' He took a sip of his drink.

'London has a lot going for it. But, to be honest, the moving around was partly an attempt to stay one step ahead of my father. It didn't work very well; he's got business interests all over Europe and it doesn't much matter where he's based as long as he's within reach of an airfield. When I went to Athens he decided to buy a house there, and when I came back to London he suddenly felt the need to return and throw a few big parties.'

'Parties?' Humour glinted in his eyes. 'Not the usual kind of parties that newly qualified doctors go to, I imagine.'

Arianna leaned towards him. It felt so natural to confide in Ben, and she wasn't sure whether it was because she owed her life to him or because he seemed to make everyone he came in contact with feel at ease.

'Nice parties. Where I could meet eligible young men who would take me away from a life of doctoring and turn me into a society lady.'

He nodded. 'I'm assuming that they didn't work so well.'

They almost had. Not quite as her father had intended, though...

Lawrence had been the antithesis of her father. He was fearless and unconventional, living for today with no thought of tomorrow. It had been refreshing at first, and he'd swept Arianna off her feet, asking her to marry him before they'd really had a chance to get to know each other. Arianna had said *yes* far too soon.

And then she'd realised. Lawrence's idea of the way they should live was really more a matter of how *he* wanted to live. His plans involved travel and spending her trust fund, and took no account of Arianna's career, because why would she want to work when she didn't have to? Even then she'd known that her work was the only stabilising factor in her life, the only reason she could find for having survived the sinking ferry when Xander hadn't.

That was all in the past now. Arianna had made her decision and her broken heart had mended, leaving her determined not to repeat her mistake. There was no going back, not on any of it.

'No. They didn't work.'

'He throws parties here?' Ben looked over his shoulder, smiling, as if he half expected to see a party heading their way.

'My father doesn't come to Ilaria...'

'Too many memories?' Something soft crept into his tone.

'Yes.' Arianna wondered how it would have been if it had been the other way around, and Xander had lived. If he'd become a doctor and come to Ilaria. Maybe her father would have come then, and maybe Xander's achievements would have meant something to her father.

'But you have your own memories, surely.'

'I love the way of life here, in the islands. I'm needed, and that's what I always wanted to be. But I chose Ilaria in particular because I thought that trying to drive my memories away wasn't the best way of dealing with them.'

'The best way isn't always the easiest.'

Arianna steeled herself against the tenderness she saw in his face. She was quite sure that if she gave into it, it would involve tears, and now wasn't the time for them. Nightmares and tears were for the darker recesses of the night.

'So…how long are you here for? Will I have an opportunity to meet your son?'

'We're here for three weeks, staying in a hotel on the mainland. Jonas is with my sister today; she's here too, with her family. I've told him all about you, though, and he'd like to meet you. I'll bring him with me the next time I come.'

'When can you come next?' Arianna pressed her lips together. Maybe she should have waited for just a few moments and made the question sound a little less a matter of life and death.

'I'm on holiday. I don't have any plans.' His melting gaze hinted at just one plan. 'Apart from coming to find you…'

He was here for *her*. No one had ever just been there for her.

The chemistry that had been flying between them fizzed and bubbled with gratification, like a test tube reaction that threatened to get out of hand and cause an explosion. Arianna's heart began to beat faster, reacting before rational thought could stop it, and she reminded herself again that acknowledging the way that Ben made her feel would be a mistake.

'I worked last weekend, so I have the day off tomorrow. Would you like to bring Jonas over to my house? We can have lunch and he can play on the beach.'

'You have your own beach?' He raised an eyebrow.

'It's…just a small one. He might like it though; it's secluded and safe for him to run around and play.'

'He'd like that. I would too, thank you. If it's not too much trouble…'

'No trouble. You could catch the morning ferry and I'll meet you at the terminus.' There was so much more that she wanted to say to Ben. Arianna wasn't sure what that was yet, but she knew she needed more time with him. A *lot* more time.

He nodded, looking at his watch and pulling a face. 'I guess we should be getting back to the health centre to see if Helen's up to the trip back tonight.'

Where had the hours gone? It didn't seem five minutes since they'd sat down at the table, but the coffee pot that the waiter had brought was empty now, and the sun had sunk low in the sky. But she had tomorrow to look forward to, and it would bring him back again.

They walked back up to the health centre together, and Arianna couldn't resist taking the route that led through the harbour and the older part of town. When Ben took a few moments to appreciate the sunset, she found herself smiling. He clearly liked Ilaria, and that meant rather more to her than it probably should.

Andreas reported back on Helen, saying that she'd been making a good recovery, and when Arianna examined her she found no trace of the painful wheeze that had accompanied her efforts to breathe earlier on. She joined Ben in the empty reception area.

'She's just getting dressed. She should be fine for the journey back. I've made sure she has a spare inhaler and I'll write a discharge note, and give you a copy. What time will you come tomorrow? There's an eleven o'clock ferry.'

There was a long night to get through before she'd see Ben again, and suddenly she wanted to know exactly how many hours she'd have to wait.

'Eleven sounds great.' He took his phone from his pocket. 'Maybe we should exchange numbers, so I can call you if we're going to be late.'

Good. Why hadn't she thought of that? Something concrete that she could take away with her. Arianna repeated her mobile number to him, hearing her phone ring as he checked he had it right. Now she had *his* number.

'Ben, I'm so glad you came. It means a lot…'

Suddenly, and without knowing quite how she'd got there, she was in his arms. She must have made the first move, Ben was still standing exactly where he had been before, but there was no mistaking his response. This felt so natural, as if time had crushed the getting-to-know-you process into a few short hours and they'd already become firm friends.

His body was strong, and as he returned the hug, she felt tears welling in her eyes. For the first time in more years than she cared to remember, she felt truly safe.

CHAPTER FOUR

'ARE WE THERE YET, DAD?'

There was a glazed glass barrier between them and the sea, but Ben still had a tight grip on his son's hand. An instinct that had survived the years since he'd seen Arianna slip under the metal railings that skirted the deck of the old ferry. That had sharpened since Emma's death.

'Not yet.' He squatted down, holding Jonas protectively against his body, and pointed into the distance. 'That's where we're going...'

Ilaria seemed to shine in the sun ahead of them. He'd texted Arianna to let her know that they were on the ferry, and she'd said she'd meet them at the terminus. Maybe she was already there, shining too.

'How *far* is it?' Jonas was clearly trying to measure the distance that the ferry still had to travel.

'About a mile.' Ben took a wild guess. 'We'll

be there soon, but we'll have to wait and take our turn to get off.'

'Okay.' The information seemed enough for the moment, and Jonas pulled away from him, staring at the island ahead of them.

Maybe fifteen minutes before he'd see Arianna again. Ben wondered whether it was possible that Jonas could be as impatient as he was. Their embrace had been echoing through his mind ever since last night.

Now that Arianna was drawing closer with every moment, he should think of it as a hug. A hug which had totally redefined the word and lasted much longer than was strictly necessary. It had said more than broken words ever could.

It had meant something more to Arianna too, he knew. When they'd heard the sound of a door opening and footsteps in the corridor that led out into the reception area, she'd pulled away from him, brushing tears from her eyes.

In that moment he'd felt something flooding back into his heart. The feeling that he wanted to protect her, and the almost painful realisation that maybe there was some way that he could. Ben hadn't allowed himself to feel that about anyone, apart from Jonas, in a very long time and it was almost as if Arianna had stripped the years away and found the man he'd once been. The one he was trying to find his way back to.

Jonas was interested in everything, the people around him, the way the ferry manoeuvred into the dock and the prospect of dry land ahead of him. Ben held his hand firmly, his gaze searching for just one person. When he saw Arianna, wearing a bright yellow sundress, his heart almost leapt into his throat. Dizzily he returned her wave, nudging at Jonas's shoulder to point her out, and the boy waved too, staring at this new person he'd heard all about.

'Hey, Jonas.' She flashed Ben a smile and then turned her attention to his son. 'Welcome to Ilaria. I'm Arianna.'

'Hello.' Jonas was a little more reserved now, watching this new person carefully. How anyone could resist the sudden sunshine of Arianna's smile was a complete mystery to Ben.

'How was the ferry ride? Did you like it?'

Jonas nodded. Arianna looked up at Ben. 'I'm parked in the harbour. I thought perhaps he'd like to have a look around there?'

'What do you think, Jonas? Shall we go and see the boats?'

Jonas perked up immediately. 'Yes, Dad!'

'Okay. The harbour it is, then.'

She seemed so keen for Jonas to like Ilaria, and for him to like her too. Arianna produced chilled drinks from the straw shopping bag she carried, smiling when Jonas accepted one from her. He'd get over his reticence soon, and then… What was not to like about Ilaria? What wasn't to love about Arianna…?

He amended the thought quickly. The 'L-word' shouldn't intrude into this equation. What wasn't to *like* about Arianna…?

By the time they reached the car, Jonas had been introduced to the men working on their boats in the harbour, and had even been allowed on one. The boy was shining with enthusiasm now, and when Arianna opened the back door of the small SUV he climbed in without a backward look at his father, getting into the child seat and waiting for Ben to strap him in.

It was only ten minutes' drive to the house, which stood in an isolated spot outside the town. When Arianna opened the front door, beckoning them inside, the interior was cool and quiet.

Inside, white-painted walls and irregular exposed stonework were given a modern feel by elegant wooden furniture and pale fabrics. At the back, shutters protected the space from the heat of the midday sun, and when Arianna opened them he saw French windows leading out onto a large patio, edged with flowering plants and shaded by a canopy draped with a vine. Beyond that, a sheltered beach and the blue of the sea.

'You have a lovely home.'

'Thank you. Shall we go outside?'

'Yes!' Jonas answered before Ben could, and Arianna smiled.

'Okay. I'll get some drinks and then you can play on the beach.' She turned to Ben. 'The bathroom's through there if you need it.'

'Thanks. I think Jonas could do with another application of sunscreen.' He pulled the bottle out of the bag he carried, along with Jonas's beach shoes.

The bathroom was white-tiled and shining. Ben stripped off Jonas's T-shirt, applying the sunscreen carefully while the boy wriggled impatiently.

He really shouldn't be noticing that only one toothbrush sat in the glass by the sink. Or imagining what it might look like with two, or three, sitting there. He wasn't looking for a relationship with anyone and, despite the instant attraction that would normally have rendered a love affair between two people practically inevitable, it was unthinkable. Guilt was a heavy burden to carry and it didn't leave much room for anyone other than Jonas in his life.

He found Arianna in the kitchen, adding sliced lemons and mint leaves to a jug of lemonade. She'd taken off her sandals, and Ben tried not to notice the natural grace of her movements, or the way the skirts of her dress moved around her bare legs.

'I'll let you choose a drink for Jonas from the fridge. There's a bottle of ouzo in there as well, if you fancy a dash to flavour the lemonade.'

'Thanks. That sounds good.' This felt like a dream. Ben hadn't allowed himself to have any expectations beyond his initial meeting with Arianna, and he wasn't sure what to say or do. Arianna seemed on edge as well.

She tipped slightly more than a dash into the pitcher, ice clanking as she mixed its contents thoroughly. Ben took a bottle of orange-flavoured water from the fridge and opened it, and Arianna leaned over, popping a bendy straw into the top of it. She opened a box of sesame and honey snacks and frowned.

'Will Jonas like these?'

'Try him.' When Arianna hesitated, Ben took two of the snacks from the box, giving one to Jonas and popping the other into his own mouth. 'Mmm... They're good...'

As he expected, Jonas followed suit and nodded his agreement. Arianna tipped the whole box into a bowl and added it to the tray that the pitcher stood on, then opened the fridge and took out two covered dishes.

'I'll put these into the oven to warm. I thought something light for now, and I'll cook later...'

'Don't go to any trouble for us, please.'

Arianna laughed suddenly and the tension between them broke, smashing into little pieces on the tiled floor.

'You're on a Greek island. You think you can sit down at *my* table without being fed?'

The warmth was back now, chasing away all the awkwardness. 'I wouldn't presume to do any such thing.'

'Good. Just as well.'

She switched the oven on, opening the kitchen door so that Ben could carry the tray out onto the patio. It was beautiful here, the breeze carrying the scent of flowers along with the tang of the sea. Sand stretched from the back of the house down to the shoreline, with raised ground and rocks on either side forming a small secluded beach. Ben took Jonas's hat from his pocket, putting it onto his son's head.

'Can I make sandcastles, Dad?' Jonas looked up at him pleadingly.

'Okay. As long as you stay where I can see you.'

'He'll be all right. This is a private beach—the land on either side of it goes with the house. I've got some buckets and spades...'

The children's buckets and spades were placed neatly in the corner of the veranda, and it was impossible that they hadn't been put there in preparation for their arrival. Ben watched as Arianna showed Jonas how to dip the buckets into the water butt at the back of the house and wet the sand a little so it would retain its shape. She was so eager to get involved, and all of Jonas's initial shyness had disappeared now and he was hanging on her every word.

He drew a line in the sand, impressing on his son that he mustn't cross it. Jonas was used to the lines that Ben drew; he'd never known anything different, and he was far too interested in his sandcastle to want to bother with the sea.

Hearing how Arianna had reacted to her own father's protectiveness was food for thought, though. It was tempting to believe he might somehow make up for Emma's death by protecting Jonas, but Ben had to admit that his solicitousness for his son was sometimes a little too much of a good thing. If Jonas reacted as Arianna had, it would break his heart.

He could think about that later, though, because right now he had a moat to dig. Jonas stood to one side, issuing instructions and advice, and then decided that if you wanted a job done well it was necessary to do it yourself.

Ben saw Arianna laughing behind her hand as Jonas relieved him of the spade and shooed him away, leaving him to walk back to the shaded patio.

'He's a great little boy. You must be very proud of him.' Arianna was watching Jonas while Ben filled two glasses from the pitcher.

'Yes, I am.' There was no hesitation in his answer. If her father had reacted in that way just once, then things might have been very different.

'It must be hard. Working and looking after him alone.'

Ben shook his head. 'It would have been harder without him. After Emma died, it was having Jonas to look after that kept me going. And I'm lucky; my sister, Lizzie, has a girl Jonas's age and she'd already made the decision to be a stay-at-home mum. She offered to look after Jonas while I was working.'

'That's a good arrangement. Although I expect he misses his mother.'

'He doesn't really remember Emma. He asks about her sometimes and we talk and look at old photographs together. I think he may start to feel her absence a little more when he's older.' Ben's brow furrowed slightly. 'I guess the two of us will deal with that when we come to it.'

Arianna guessed they would too. Her own loss seemed so long ago in comparison and not nearly as life-changing, but somehow Ben had managed to look forward. Maybe she should take a leaf from his book and shake off her nightmares.

Their conversation drifted, past places they both knew in London, and things they'd both done as doctors. When the timer sounded from the kitchen Arianna jumped to her feet, hurrying inside, and then reappeared with a bowl of warm *tiropita* in one hand and one of *keftedakia* in the other. Ben called Jonas, taking him into the kitchen to wash his hands.

Jonas worked his way through everything that was put in front of him, and then ran back to his castle. Arianna made coffee, and they watched Jonas playing in the sand. When he called his father, Ben slipped off his shoes to walk out onto the beach and Arianna followed him.

'That's amazing. Fantastic work, Jonas. What do you think, Arianna?'

'Best I've ever seen.'

Ben rolled up his trouser legs and knelt down in the sand next to his son, and the boy nestled close. 'That's a great moat. Like the one we saw at Leeds Castle.'

Jonas wrinkled his nose. 'It doesn't have any water, Dad. And I can't go across the line.' He pointed at the line that Ben had drawn in the sand.

'Yeah, good boy. It's okay if you and I go across the line together. Perhaps we'll just flatten the sand a bit first, eh?'

Ben started to tamp down the sand at the bottom of the moat and Jonas followed suit, watching his father carefully. Arianna knelt down on the other side.

'Can I help?' Maybe this was something that Ben and Jonas wanted to do together.

'Hear that? Your castle has its very own princess who doesn't mind getting her hands dirty.' Ben grinned at Jonas. 'I think that'll be a yes please, won't it?'

'Yes! You can do that bit.' Jonas pointed to a segment next to his own. 'Please…'

She could feel Jonas's warm skin against her arm as they worked. His hands pressing on top of hers. The half-remembered feeling of playing with other kids, before she'd lost her childhood and become the little girl who made no noise, and who didn't attract any attention to herself, for fear that the weight of her parents' grief might suddenly break free and crush her.

'Dad…' Jonas frowned. 'You have to do the sides too. *We're* doing the sides.'

'Yep. In a minute. I'll just finish off here…' Ben was packing the sand down at the bottom of the moat first, and Jonas clearly felt that his father wasn't doing things in the right order. Wriggling in between Ben's arms, Jonas started to rectify the problem, tamping the sand at the sides.

Arianna left them, nudging each other good-naturedly out of the way, and went to fetch three large buckets. Ben got to his feet, catching two of the buckets up in his hand, while Jonas followed suit, picking up the two small children's pails. When they got to the line in the sand, he slid one foot over it, grinning cheekily up at his dad, and Ben laughed, picking him up and swinging him over the line, before racing him down to the water's edge. When Jonas reached the sea, he dropped his pails and started to splash water at his father.

'So *that's* the way you want it, eh?' Ben growled, lifting his son up into the air and then threatening to dunk him in the waves.

Jonas shrieked with joy, his arms and legs flailing, and as Ben lowered him he sent a plume of water in his father's direction, hitting him full in the face. Arianna heard herself laugh.

Two blond heads turned in her direction. Jonas flung his arms above his head, beckoning to her to join the game. Ben's smile was less demonstrative, but much more compelling.

Could she cross the line in the sand? The line that had been drawn when her brother died and she'd suddenly been sucked into the emptiness of a family bound by grief. Arianna had thought that the chance to play with other kids was long gone now, but Ben's smile was irresistible…

She walked down to the water's edge and, as soon as she was in range, Jonas sent a splash of water in her direction. She side-stepped out of the way and Ben picked Jonas up, holding him clear of the water.

'Careful, mate. Don't get Arianna's dress all wet.'

Suddenly, she didn't care about that. Arianna gathered her skirts up in one hand, wading into the water and sending a splash in Jonas's direction, then another larger one towards Ben.

'Hey! How come I'm so wet…?'

Because…he looked so much better wet than dry. His T-shirt was sticking to his skin, clearly outlining an impressive pair of shoulders. The temptation to run her fingers across his chest, to see if it felt as good as it looked, was almost too much. His blue eyes were ninety per cent laughter but the other ten per cent were all smouldering heat, which burned right into her soul.

Jonas had decided to even the odds a little,

and when his father let him down into the water he filled one of his pails, running over to his father and drenching him.

'Uh…two can play at that game…' Ben filled one of the larger buckets and Jonas ran squealing away to hide behind Arianna.

One look from those mischievous blue eyes that seemed entirely for her, and all about play of a much more adult nature. Then he stepped back, filling the other bucket and walking away up the beach, leaving Arianna to help Jonas dunk his pails into the sea. He gave her one to carry, taking her hand as they walked back to the sandcastle.

Ben carefully emptied the water into the moat, grinning as he passed them on his way back down to the sea. Sudden blinding desire gripped her, and she tried to focus her eyes on his face. But she couldn't resist turning to watch him for just a moment, before Jonas tugged on her hand, impatient to add their water to the moat.

When she looked again towards the water's edge, she saw that Ben had stripped off his T-shirt and was wringing it out in the sea, sunshine glistening on his skin. Its warm fingers seemed to caress him as he moved, and Arianna froze.

'We need more water.' Jonas nudged her and she jumped, pulled back into the moment.

'Yes, we do.' Arianna reached for the last bucket, grabbing her sunglasses at the same time and settling them firmly on her nose. They were a meagre enough defence against the golden lines of Ben's body, but at least it wasn't quite so obvious that she couldn't drag her gaze away from him.

As she walked back down the beach with Jonas, Ben flapped his T-shirt in the breeze and pulled it back over his head. That didn't help as much as it should have done; his image was already burned into her mind. He gave her a cheery smile, dodging out of the way as Jonas splashed more water in his direction, and filling the buckets in the sea.

When the moat was full, and Jonas was busily engaged in building a causeway across it made from stones and shells, Ben came to sit next to her on the steps that ran down from the veranda.

'Would you like a towel?' He smelled of sun, sand and the sea. Like the faraway, much missed summers that she'd spent with her family, here on the island.

'No, I'm fine, thank you. Almost dry now.'

She'd noticed. Had watched as dry patches appeared on his T-shirt, wanting to trace their edges with her finger. They'd spread and begun to join and now she could almost... almost look at him without feeling that her heart was going to stop.

'Your practice here is very different from mine.' He leaned back on his elbows, basking in the sun. 'Different and yet the same.'

'Yes. Some of the problems are unique, but many of them are the same as the ones I saw when I was working in London. I learned a lot there.'

He nodded. 'My practice would kill for the kind of facilities you have here, at the health centre. But it's a lot easier for me to send people to the hospital for things like blood tests and X-rays.'

'That's true.' Arianna quirked her lips down. 'Although we do have better facilities than some island practices.'

He raised an eyebrow, but didn't ask. Arianna couldn't help answering anyway. There was no holding out against a man who combined beauty and brains.

'When I came here there was no doctor, and no medical centre. If someone was ill they had to go to the mainland. There were funds available to start up a practice, but we would have had to raise a lot more money to afford anything approaching what we have now. Then an...anonymous donor made a very large gift.'

Ben nodded slowly. 'That sounds extremely well timed.' The humour in his eyes left Arianna in no doubt that he'd put two and two together and that four was the correct answer.

'Doesn't it. My father had just about come around to the idea that I was serious about being a doctor, and had been hoping I'd opt for a smart practice in Athens when I came back to Greece. He knew I couldn't turn the donation down.'

'Because it wasn't really for you; it was for your patients.'

'Yes. When I told him I knew it was him, he said that he wanted me to have a nice place to work. Although, if that was all he'd wanted, he could have spent a great deal less.'

'So it was an altruistic move, after all?'

'My father does care about Ilaria. Did you notice that the harbour was a little different when you arrived yesterday?'

He shook his head. 'I noticed that nothing seemed familiar. I was only here for less than a day and it was a long time ago.'

It seemed like yesterday. But it *had* been a long time.

'The ferry that we were on was hit by a larger ferry that had just left the harbour. It had always been a bit of a tight squeeze for the ferries to get in and out of the bay, and my father had a separate ferry terminal built, so that things were much safer for both the ferries and the smaller boats in the harbour. Two men from here drowned as well as my brother, and he made sure that their families would always be provided for. He built the hotel on the other side of the island as well, which has provided employment and allowed people to stay on the island.'

'So he does his good deeds by stealth.' Ben smiled.

'By chequebook. He doesn't turn up in person.'

'Never?'

'No. I didn't expect him to buy a house here and start throwing parties, the way he did in London, but I'd hoped he might finally decide to come back. But he hasn't set foot on the island since the day of the ferry accident. I haven't seen him in two years.'

Ben was watching Jonas playing in the sand, his expression tight and pinched suddenly. Arianna wondered if there was anything that could ever keep him from his son. Maybe if Jonas became an astronaut and flew to Mars…

'Coming here must have been challenging for you.'

'Yes and no. When I first got here, I had to work very hard to oversee the building works for the health centre, and to gain people's confidence. Most of the older people here remember me as a child, and everyone knows what happened, but it took a while to convince them that I could be their doctor.'

He nodded. 'Yeah, *busy* can carry you through a lot of things. It did me, when Emma died, but as soon as I caught my breath I realised I was only postponing the loss I needed to feel.'

Maybe that was what she'd done too. Arianna hadn't told anyone about the nightmares, and after all this time no one had asked. But she couldn't shake the certainty that Ben just knew.

'You had nightmares?' She couldn't look at him for fear that he'd see her own reflecting in her eyes.

'Yes.'

'And they passed?'

'Yes. They did.' His voice seemed to pull her back out of the vortex and offer her a way forward. Maybe if she just clung to him…

Or maybe if she stood on her own two feet and pulled herself together. That was Arianna's preferred coping strategy and it generally worked.

'Good. That's good.' She let out a breath and got to her feet. 'I should make a start on lunch. Is there anything that Jonas doesn't like?'

'He's at the stage where he's beginning to like trying new things.'

'Jonas…' she called over to the boy. 'What's your favourite food?'

'Fingers and chips,' he answered straight-away.

'That's fish fingers and chips.' Ben grinned,

beckoning to his son. 'Happy to try something different?'

'Yes.' Jonas's dirty hands found their way onto his father's knees. 'Dad says it's okay if I try something and don't like it because he eats it.'

'But if you have fingers and chips, your dad goes hungry?'

Jonas nodded solemnly and Ben chuckled, pulling a face of exaggerated dismay.

'I'll go and see if I have some fish fingers in my freezer then.'

CHAPTER FIVE

IT HAD SEEMED almost inevitable that they should find something to bring them together again. Sun, sand and sea had done its work yesterday, and Ben had stayed longer at Arianna's than he'd meant to, the two of them talking on the veranda until it was time to hurry down to catch the last ferry.

And today it would be their work. Ben's questions about Arianna's practice had finally led her to laugh, shake her head to catch the sun in her curls and tell him that he could see for himself. A visiting doctor could observe, even if the necessary paperwork to allow him to practise wasn't in place. It had been approximately fourteen hours since Ben had seen her last, and already he'd started to miss her.

She was a mass of inconsistencies. Vulnerable and yet capable, impulsive but measured. Her feet were planted firmly on the ground, yet she was capable of dreaming. Arianna's beauty was the only thing about her that wasn't tempered by an opposite balancing force. His fascination with her was getting to be much the same, never wavering in its intensity.

Maybe that was to be expected. It was as if they'd been fused together that day on the ferry, and then both spent twenty-five years wondering what had become of the other. That twenty-five years hadn't been as straightforward as either of them might have hoped, but Ben had realised that the one constant thing in his life had been his wish to find Arianna again.

'There!' Jonas had been playing a game with Ben's sister, Lizzie, pointing out every young woman with dark hair who entered the hotel coffee shop and trying to make Lizzie guess whether it was Arianna or not. This time the word was accompanied by a chuckle, and Ben looked up.

Arianna's dress was a mixture of reds and pinks today, and she wore a pair of red deck shoes. She shone, as she always did, and his heart lurched in response. As it always seemed to whenever she was around.

She gave Jonas a wave, and the boy ran to her for a hug. Arianna's awkward delight showed on her face. What kind of fractures had split her own family that she was so unused to the normal ebullience of a child? Ben set the thought aside and smiled up at her.

'You're early. Do you have time to join us for coffee?'

Arianna looked at her watch and sat down in the empty chair next to his. 'Yes, I think I do.'

He left Jonas to introduce her to Lizzie, her husband, James, and their three children, and signalled to the waiter. By the time everyone had decided what they wanted, Arianna and Lizzie had already started chatting.

'It's a shame we didn't get a booking for the hotel on the island.' Lizzie turned the corners of her mouth down. 'Ben wouldn't hear of it, but now it's a bit of a trek backwards and forwards for you both.'

Arianna turned her gaze onto him. 'It would have been a lot more convenient.'

'As things have turned out. I didn't know

whether you'd even want to see me, let alone if you'd want me staying on the island for three weeks.'

'Perhaps we could get a swap. I think this hotel's run by the same group as the one on the island,' Lizzie interjected helpfully, blithely unaware that she was sitting with the daughter of the man who owned both hotels. 'What do you reckon?'

James nodded, obviously happy to go with the flow, and suddenly all eyes were on Ben. The idea of moving to the island had occurred to him as well, but he'd far rather have spoken to Arianna about it alone first.

'I'm…um… Perhaps it's better to stay where we are.'

Arianna's face fell. He'd said the wrong thing.

'Or we *could* move.'

'I think it would be better to move, if we can.' Lizzie was committed to the plan already. 'What do you think, Arianna?'

'I know the manager of the hotel on the island. I'd be happy to ask if he can arrange something and you can go from there.'

The idea was agreed, but Ben decided he

would find out how Arianna really felt about it later. Because she had already moved on, asking Lizzie where they'd been and what they were planning to do today, and the conversation lasted until their coffee cups were empty.

Ben looked at his watch. 'Should we be going?'

'Oh.' Arianna looked at hers. 'Yes, I think we should…'

She stifled a yawn as they walked out of the hotel and into the bright sunshine, and they walked silently towards the hotel's marina. Suddenly she seemed tired, and Ben remembered that she'd asked him about nightmares. He wondered if the question was a little more personal to her than he'd supposed, and how much she'd slept last night.

She stopped by the neat blue and white boat that she'd pointed out yesterday in the harbour as belonging to the health centre. Something was clearly on her mind.

'If you don't want to stay on Ilaria…' Her lip quivered almost imperceptibly, but Ben had now become used to watching everything about her.

'I just didn't want you to feel crowded.'

Right answer. She smiled again, the lines of fatigue disappearing from her face.

'I don't. It'll be nice to have you and your family there. The hotel has a lovely beach, which isn't as busy as the one here. It's a little more orientated towards relaxing, while this one is better if you want to go sightseeing.'

He reached for her, and suddenly the world around them faded into the background and they were alone on the jetty. His fingers skimming the warm skin of her arm were the only thing that seemed to matter.

She felt it too. Arianna let out the merest hint of a gasp, looking up at him. Locked in the warmth of her eyes, it felt like an embrace. A kiss. The very sweetest one imaginable.

'Lizzie and James can relax, and the kids can play on the beach. What *I'd* really like to do is spend more time with you.'

Her reply was in her eyes. Warm and bright, with the hint of a tear. Someone brushed against her back, and as Ben stretched out his arm instinctively to protect her the moment was shattered.

'I'll…um…give the manager a call, then. I'm sure he can sort out something.'

'You're sure? You've worked hard to make sure that everyone on the island sees you for what you are, and not who your father is. We're not asking for any favours.'

Again, that warmth in her eyes made Ben want to lean in and hold her close. Protect her from all the hurt she seemed to carry with her.

'That's okay. I've never asked the manager for anything before. I imagine he'll be relieved that he has something to report back on to my father.'

Ben raised his eyebrows. 'People report back on you?'

Arianna shrugged. 'I'm sure it's not written into his job description, but my father does always seem to know what I'm up to. It's his way of caring… From a distance.'

She turned suddenly, stepping confidently onto the boat before Ben could extend his hand to steady her. Arianna handed him a life jacket and smilingly refused his help in slipping the mooring lines, before she carefully manoeuvred away from the dock.

'How often do you visit Kantos?' The island was visible on the horizon already, as the boat sped across the blue water.

'I have a surgery there on Mondays and Fridays, and Andreas goes across every Wednesday. And there's a full-time pharmacist on the island as well; he often deals with day-to-day problems. I don't have too many people to see this morning, so maybe we'll have a chance to go up to the Lava Lake afterwards.'

The famous Lava Lake of Kantos was on Ben's list of places to see. Seeing it with Arianna put it firmly at the top of said list.

She steered the boat into the little harbour at Kantos, mooring it. Ben picked up her medical bag and they walked together through the narrow sun-baked streets.

'Here we are…' She unlocked the door of a stone-built house which stood some way back from the road. Inside, the rooms were shaded and cool and a little old-fashioned.

'Waiting room…' Arianna pointed to a large room at the front, decorated with dark wooden furniture and seats arranged in groups. 'My surgery…'

The surgery was at the back of the building.

A large mahogany desk and a heavy bookcase gave it an air of gravitas, and when Arianna opened the heavily shaded doors at the back, the light streaming in and her own bright dress added a note of exuberance.

'You're sure you want to sit in on my surgery? You *are* on holiday, and there's a nice taverna in the harbour...'

'If you don't mind. The holiday part is that I'm not responsible for any of your patients.'

'I don't mind at all.' She pulled a heavy leather upholstered chair across the room, positioning it next to hers. Ben grinned at her, pulling the chair back into the corner, and she laughed. 'Okay. Be a fly on the wall.'

It was both the same and different. The differences were immediately obvious. There was no receptionist and when Arianna rang the buzzer to usher a new patient into the surgery, the waiting room just produced the next in line by consensus. She smilingly explained that everyone knew everyone anyway, and that those who couldn't wait were given priority by the others. Jumping the queue was out of the question, and anyone who did that would never hear the last of it.

She knew everyone. Ben couldn't follow the conversations, but she greeted everyone by name without looking at her notes, and when she tilted her head, obviously asking each new person how they were keeping, the long replies seemed to include information of a social nature as well as medical details. Some patients were given stern instructions, accompanied by a look that implied Arianna would be checking up on them afterwards. Others were quietly reassured. In his own practice, and with the best will in the world, Ben couldn't even recognise all of his patients, and only knew their names and some very basic personal details by scanning the computer while they were on their way to his surgery. His approach was necessarily reactive, while Arianna's was more proactive.

One elderly man saw Ben sitting in the corner and insisted on directing his explanations of his medical condition at him instead of Arianna. She waited, arms folded, until he'd finished speaking and gesturing at his left arm, which appeared to Ben to have limited mobility. Something told him that she was well in charge of the situation and that there was no need to intervene, and her murmured words seemed to set things straight. The man turned to her and went through the gestures all over again.

'What did you say to him?' Ben asked while the waiting room was deciding on the next patient.

'I said that you were assisting me today, and that you didn't know everyone's medical history. If he wasn't careful you might try to get him to raise his arm above his head.' She grinned at Ben and suddenly the world seemed to tip a little, as if he were being sucked into the mischief in her dark eyes.

'Ouch. Frozen shoulder?'

'Yes. Do you mind my saying you were my assistant?'

Not in the slightest. Arianna's way of managing her patients was both efficient and charming. He'd be her assistant any day.

'It's a promotion from fly-on-the-wall. I'm extremely happy with it…'

He settled back into his seat as the next patient arrived. For all the differences and personal touches, Arianna's practice was much the same as his. She was thorough and capable, the kind of doctor that everyone aspired to be. But, unlike him, she wasn't one part of a greater machine that provided him with support and backup. She'd achieved all of this by herself.

Ben's Greek extended to 'please' and 'thank you,' and he clearly didn't understand the word *sýzygos*. That was a relief, because it had passed the lips of more than one of her patients this afternoon. Yes, he was undoubtedly good husband material. And no, his name wasn't on her list of prospective husbands because, believe it or not, and most people didn't, she didn't possess such a list.

It was nice having him here, though. He had obviously divined what ailed a number of her patients, just from watching her examinations, but he didn't interrupt with any of his own observations. Compared with her father's constant questions about whether she knew what she was doing with her life, it was a welcome show of respect.

'So.' She turned to him as the last patient closed the door of the surgery behind her. 'What do you think?'

'I think you're making a difference.'

'It's not exactly cutting-edge medicine.' Arianna wondered how he would respond to her father's assertion, that if she was going to work for a living she should choose something a little more high-profile. Or at least some*where* a little more high-profile, like the city.

Ben winced. 'What do you want me to say? I'm a working GP too, so clearly I think that this makes a difference. What I see here is that if I had the ability to know my patients a little better, then I could make more of the kind of difference you're making here.'

'Okay.' Arianna held her hands up in an expression of willing defeat. 'What I actually wanted you to say was that it doesn't matter where you practice. Now you're telling me that it does and that I'm doing better than you.'

He chuckled. 'Fair enough. It doesn't matter where you practice, then. You're still doing more for your patients than I can. Are you ready to go now? I'm looking forward to seeing the Lava Lake.'

The conversation was turning into a flirtation, possibly because Ben's smile made everything a flirtation, and possibly because of the warm feeling that his approval gave. Arianna's phone rang and she picked it up from the desk, watching as Ben turned towards the window, staring outside to the large garden at the back, where Mrs Kyriakou and her daughter Athena were bidding their goodbyes to the last of the children they'd been minding while their mothers were visiting the surgery.

The message being relayed to her was the last thing she wanted to hear right now. The Lava Lake, along with Ben, started to recede from her immediate future.

'Ben, I'm sorry but the Lava Lake's going to have to wait. I'll find someone to take you back to Ilaria—something's come up.'

'What's happened?' He was suddenly alert.

'There's been an accident on one of the fishing boats. I have to take the boat out to meet them.'

'Can I help? I'm assuming you have no other medical staff available.'

'Are you sure…?' Arianna swallowed down the objection that Ben was on holiday because she really could use his help. 'I can't wait for Andreas to get here; it'll take him too long.'

'Then let's go.'

Ben carried Arianna's medical bag as they both hurried down to the harbour. A young man was waiting for them at the dock, and Arianna translated what he said for Ben as they all climbed into the boat.

'They're drifting, somewhere over there.' She pointed towards a clear expanse of sea. 'They had engine problems and a couple of the crew have been hurt, so we'll need to give them a tow as well. Georgios is coming with us, to help.'

At the mention of his name, Georgios held out his hand to Ben and the men nodded a hello. Then he turned to stand with Arianna at the helm, obviously giving her directions. When a fishing boat became visible, Georgios took out his phone, obviously speaking to the people on board and then relaying the gist of the conversation to Arianna.

'Well, they're not sinking, so that's good news.' Arianna was staring ahead of her as she steered towards the boat. 'I think the best thing for us to do is to go across onto the fishing boat and see how badly the men are injured, while Georgios sorts out a towing line.'

'Okay. Just tell me what to do and when to do it.' Ben smiled at her. Arianna was confident and capable, and there was no trace of hesitation in her manner. Clearly she remembered the panic and confusion of the ferry, but it seemed she'd put it behind her and had no fear of the water now.

She manoeuvred the boat alongside the fishing boat, a larger wooden craft with a small cabin towards the back and nets tumbled across the deck at the front, as if they'd been hauled in with haste. One man sat alone, nursing his arm, and the other four were clustered around a prone figure.

He clambered up onto the fishing boat, turning to help Arianna. But she was already beside him, stretching down as Georgios passed her medical bag up to her. Above the clamour of the sea there was no sound other than the moans of the stricken man. Ben's gaze caught Arianna's and she nodded in silent agreement. There was a different note to the cries of a patient in crisis, and it sounded as if someone had been badly hurt.

'If you take a look at the man sitting over there…' She looked around, motioning over to one of the fishermen. 'Dimitris speaks a bit of English. Best we can do, I'm afraid… If you need splints or a sling, there are some in the long chest on the left, in the cabin of my boat.'

'That's great, thanks.' Arianna had given him all he needed, despite the almost unbearable feeling that he should stay with her, be there for her, Ben knew that a division of labour was best for their patients. She'd call him if she needed him. He hoped.

It turned out to be easier just to motion to the man with the injured arm, as Dimitris's attempts at translation weren't all that intelligible. A careful examination showed that the man had a nasty fracture of his forearm, and Ben climbed back onto Arianna's boat and found an emergency splint and a sling. He'd leave pain relief to Arianna; the labels on all the drugs packages were in Greek and although he was pretty sure of what everything was, he couldn't be positive.

Meanwhile, Arianna had called to Georgios and a burns kit was being handed up onto the fishing boat. Not good news. Ben went back to his own patient, carefully inflating the splint around the fracture and positioning the arm in a sling. That should make him more comfortable until they could get him to a hospital, and a thumbs-up and a smile told him that the man was feeling better.

'Anything else?' Ben hoped that Dimitris would be able to translate that correctly, and looked at a small cut on his patient's cheek. The blood was already congealing and there was nothing to suggest any further injury.

'No. *Entáxei…* Okay.' Dimitris glanced over to where Arianna was kneeling over the other man, rapping out instructions in Greek. 'Go… Go help.'

'All right. You stay here. Watch him…' Words and gestures made Ben's meaning clear and Dimitris nodded, sitting down next to their patient. Finally Ben allowed himself to turn away.

Arianna glanced up at him. 'His leg is badly scalded by steam from the engine. We can't tow the fishing boat back; we'll have to take him on my boat, straight over to the mainland. I've called for an ambulance and they'll meet us back at the hotel marina.'

Ben nodded. 'What do you want me to do?'

'I'm going to get some pain relief for him; will you finish the dressings, please?' Arianna was carefully applying cooling gel dressings to the angry-looking burns that ran from the man's ankle to above his knee.

'Will do.' Ben stripped off his surgical gloves, putting on a new pair from the burns kit. 'While you're about it, the other guy has a fractured arm. I haven't given him anything, and I've no idea whether or not he's taken anything already.'

Arianna nodded. 'Okay, leave it with me. I'll be back in a minute.'

She spoke to her patient, then got to her feet, stepping back down onto the smaller craft that bobbed in the sea next to the fishing boat. Ben finished applying the dressings, keeping a close eye on his face. The man was clearly in a lot of pain and, although the area covered by the burn wasn't enough to make hypovolemic shock likely, he was clearly emotionally traumatised by his injury, and that could well provoke a sudden reaction.

Arianna returned and administered a pain-killing injection, then walked over to their other patient to check on how he was doing. Georgios passed a stretcher up to the men on the fishing boat, and then caught a line that was thrown down, pulling the two boats together until they were almost touching.

They worked together silently, Arianna finishing the dressings while Ben assembled the stretcher. When their patient was lifted onto it, he groaned in pain and Ben set about packing a blanket around his shoulders and body.

'Is that…?' He nodded towards the men, who were now lashing the boats together. Ben wasn't quite sure how this was going to work.

'It'll be fine. These men live on the water; they know how to get a stretcher from one boat to another. Just stay back and do as you're told.' She grinned at him suddenly.

'Aye-aye, Captain.' Ben shot her a smile, the warmth of the afternoon tingling through his body.

He stood back and did as he was told. Georgios helped the man with the broken arm into

a seat and strapped him in, and Arianna secured the stretcher under the sheltered aw-
ning at the front of the boat.

'The blood pressure monitor's in there.' She
pointed to one of the chests that lined the
cabin. 'Will you keep an eye on him, please?'

Ben nodded. Arianna slid behind the wheel,
checking that none of the ropes that secured
them to the fishing boat were still in place,
and started the engine. They left the stranded
fishing boat, the men lined up along the side
watching the boat as it headed for the mainland.

The man on the stretcher groaned and
retched. The small cabin didn't give him
space to turn him on his side without compromising the careful protection around his leg,
and Ben sat him up. Arianna's concentration
didn't waver as she carefully navigated the
waters that were becoming more and more
crowded as they neared the mainland. She
manoeuvred into the marina, and Ben saw
an ambulance waiting for them.

The Greek paramedics who met them were
part of one of the best health services in Europe.
They were well trained and well equipped, lift-

ing the burns victim out of the boat and into the ambulance quickly. Arianna briefed them on his treatment so far, while Ben helped the other man off the boat and to the back doors of the ambulance.

'*Efcharistó.*' The man held out his uninjured hand to Ben and he took it.

'You're welcome. Take care.' Ben didn't know how to say that in Greek, although he understood the *thank you*. It didn't seem to matter, though, and when one of the ambulance crew came to guide the man into the vehicle, he stopped to shake his hand again.

'Right then.' Arianna jumped down from the ambulance and the back doors closed. 'I suppose we should go and see if the fishing boat still needs a tow.'

There was something brittle about her smile. After her calm efficiency with their patients, the flashed smiles that told him she was happy with the way they'd just fallen into a rhythm of working together, it was slightly odd. When she went to the boat she handed the ignition keys to Georgios, and when the two men made for the cabin, Arianna loitered at the back of the boat, sitting down alone.

He should leave her. Maybe she *did* have qualms about being on the water after all, and they'd just been submerged in her wish to get to an injured man as quickly as possible. She seemed to want to be alone with her thoughts for a moment and Ben stood next to Georgios, his gaze fixed on the stranded fishing boat ahead of them.

But she was always there. Not just as a bright splash of colour on the edge of his vision, but hovering in his thoughts as he helped Georgios secure the towline, and then moved back up to the front of the boat again. Their progress was slower now, and he watched the small harbour of Kantos, which seemed a lot busier than it had been when they'd left, with people gathering on the dock to find out what had happened at sea.

Arianna was all activity again, jumping off the boat before Georgios had a chance to fix the mooring lines, and making a beeline for a group that was standing together at the end of the quay. She spoke to them intently, and Ben saw her reach for the hands of one of the women. These must be the families of the injured men.

Willing hands reached to catch the mooring lines from the fishing boat. The men joined their families, and in the noise of conversation and questions that he could neither understand nor answer he caught sight of Arianna, surrounded by people.

He wanted to make sure she was all right, but he had to wait his turn. Many of the villagers wanted to speak to Arianna and shake her hand, and when he pushed his way through the gathering crowd he could feel people clapping him on the back.

'Let's get out of here...' She flashed him a tight smile when she saw him, and Ben wondered whether that was a suggestion or a plea. He cleared a path for her through people who were milling around them and she followed, silent now and without the smiles that had accompanied her conversations with the families of the men on the fishing boat.

Ben headed for the shaded surgery, knowing that was probably the one place that they could be alone.

CHAPTER SIX

THE NIGHTMARES THAT had been kept at bay for so long had begun to gain focus. As Arianna had begun to relax after the hard work of building her practice they'd become more frequent, and now...

Now they were starting to leak out into her days. Last night they'd been terrifyingly clear and when she'd gone down to the harbour this morning, the sound of the ferry horn had made her jump. The bobbing motion of her own boat had brought tears to her eyes, and then she'd brushed them away, telling herself that she'd see Ben soon.

His presence, and then the urgency of their mission to the stranded boat, had chased her fears away. But as soon as they'd left the injured men on the mainland and she had time to think again, she'd felt suddenly sick, pointless questions echoing in her head. What if...? What if somehow she could go back through time, and the doctor's boat could provide willing hands to pull her brother from the water? Her father had built a new dock for the ferry, to make sure that day could never happen again. She'd come here to make sure that there would be medical help available without having to send to the mainland. None of it seemed enough, because nothing could prevent what had already happened.

Ben walked beside her, back to the surgery, without saying a word. There was something companionable in the silence, as if he understood everything that she was feeling. Even if that was comforting, Arianna desperately needed *someone* to understand and it felt that Ben, or at least her own fantasy of him, always *had* understood her.

She made it to the building that housed the surgery, proud of the way that her hand was steady when she took the keys from her bag and unlocked the door. Good. Fine. She was doing okay. Her footsteps sounded on the tiled floor and she opened the door into the surgery. Light slanted through the blinds, the same way that it had filtered down through the water when she'd found herself sinking beneath the waves…

'Hey, there.' She felt Ben's arms around her shoulders and squeezed her eyes shut.

'I'm not crying…'

'No. Of course you're not. Never occurred to me that you were.'

Okay, so she *was* crying. And her limbs were shaking too, against the quiet strength of his body.

'I'm fine. Really. Pretend it didn't happen.'

She felt his chest heave in a sigh. 'Pretend *what* didn't happen? The whole of the last twenty-five years?'

That was the glue that held them together. A lifetime that had been spent dealing with the fallout of what had happened that day on the ferry, and Ben's uncanny ability to understand that. His life had been changed by that day as well.

'I'm just… This is crazy.' She pulled away from him, wiping her eyes. 'I'm not going to dwell on the past, Ben. I've never done that.'

He nodded. The smile that hovered at the corners of his mouth had a hint of reproach in it.

'What?' Whatever it was, he might as well just come out and say it.

'You've told me your whole life story, and you've not once been sorry for yourself…'

Arianna frowned at him. 'There's a *but* in there, isn't there.'

'You want to hear this?'

No. Something told her that she really, really didn't want to hear it. But his eyes were mesmerising, and they wouldn't let her go.

'Probably not. Say it anyway.'

'I think you've worked hard and that you're making a difference, but you can't enjoy that because you're still the little girl who's so bound up with her parents' grief that she won't show her own. You're still trying to prove to everyone that you're not the second-best child who survived, but you can't prove it to yourself.'

The emotion swelled inside her.

'How dare you?' Before Arianna knew what she was doing she'd raised her hand, ready to slap him. He didn't even flinch and that somehow made her behaviour even worse. Tears of frustration started to well in her eyes and she brushed them away impatiently.

'I'm sorry, Ben. This isn't all about me, I know that.'

'Do it.' His eyes taunted her. 'It would be the first really honest thing you've done.'

'I don't know what you mean by that.'

'Sure you do. Do it.' He stuck his chin out, pointing at it. 'Right there.'

'No. I'm not going to hit you.'

'Not even if I tell you to grow up. Face your grief and admit that you're *not* second-best, that's just survivor's guilt talking...'

He stepped back as Arianna flung herself at him, catching her flailing arms. Held her while she cried bitter tears and was still there for her when she wiped her face with shaking fingers. For a long time they were both silent, locked in an embrace. Held together by the day they'd met, when they were both children.

He reached into his pocket, bringing out a handkerchief. Wiping her face gently and carefully was more than just wiping the tears away; it felt as if he were cleaning away the remains of the shell that had kept her imprisoned for so long.

'I didn't think men carried handkerchiefs

these days...' She took the scrap of cloth from his fingers, blowing her nose. 'Isn't it a little old-fashioned, having a hanky in your pocket just in case you come across a woman in distress?'

'A hanky comes in very useful when you have a five-year-old. Scraped knees, dirty face, runny nose. It's as well that I haven't been around Jonas too much today, or you wouldn't want to be blowing your nose on it.'

Arianna smiled, putting the handkerchief in her pocket. 'I'll wash it and give it back to you.'

He chuckled. 'Now who's the old-fashioned one?'

Ben took her hand, wrapping his fingers around it. 'I know that my coming here has brought up some very difficult issues for you, Arianna. I'm sorry, and if you'd like me to leave...'

'No.' She laid her finger across his lips.

'You don't have to put a brave face on things, or keep up appearances. If I'm making things worse for you, you don't have to pretend you want me around either.'

She could ask Ben. She really *wanted* to ask

him. No one had ever been able to see into her heart the way he seemed to, and it was terrifying and yet liberating.

'I'd like you to stay.'

'Then I'll stay.' His gaze focused on her face and he tilted her jaw upwards with one finger. 'How much sleep did you get last night?'

'Is that a nice way of saying I have bags under my eyes?'

He grinned. 'I have to look really, really closely to see them. How much?'

'Not a lot.' Arianna turned the corners of her mouth down. The nightmares had been clearer and more disturbing than ever, and in the end she'd wrapped herself in a blanket and sat outside, watching the sun rise.

'What do you say to my cooking for you tonight, then? You can sit on the veranda and watch the sunset.'

'That sounds good. If you're sure, though. You're on holiday, so you should be the one that has the time to sit around watching sunsets.'

His face creased into a pained expression. 'I came here to see you, Arianna. I didn't know what to expect, but if I'd wanted to just laze in the sun then I'd have gone somewhere else.'

'How are you with a barbecue, then?'

He laid his hand on his chest. 'If Jonas were here, he'd tell you. You're looking at the barbecue king.'

Ben shooed Arianna out of her own kitchen and he saw her pick up her phone and take it with her onto the veranda. She sat down, curling her legs up under her, and dialled, speaking in Greek to someone. He heard Lizzie's name mentioned, and guessed that Arianna must be talking about their hotel transfer. Ben turned away from the window and started to unpack the bags of food they'd brought from the village. Chicken for the barbecue, and salad.

The barbecue was housed in its own covered area, to one side of the veranda and outside the kitchen. This was outdoor living at its very best. Shaded places to cook and eat, and the beach and the sunshine to enjoy. Ben could get used to this.

He laid the table on the veranda, and then brought out the dishes of food.

'Very nice. You can come back again.' She smiled at him. Arianna still looked tired, but the light had returned to her dark eyes and she seemed less careworn.

'Thanks. Next time it's pie and chips.'

'Pie and chips is fine. I used to live in London too, remember? Or do you do sausages and mash?'

'Definitely. With homemade onion gravy.'

Arianna grinned and sat down at the table. 'I'm going to need to try that before you go.'

They spent a lazy hour, talking and eating, as the sun went down. Ben had reminded Arianna not to move while he cleared away the plates and made coffee, and he was stacking the dishwasher when his phone rang.

'That was Lizzie,' he called to her from the kitchen door after he hung up. 'She says that the manager of our hotel has arranged for us to move across to the island first thing tomorrow morning.'

'That's good.' Arianna didn't seem much surprised by the news.

'Yeah. I don't suppose you had anything

to do with our being upgraded to a suite, did you?' Ben felt slightly uncomfortable about that.

'It was what they had available. There's a similar suite in all of my father's hotels, which is used for family and friends. It's usually empty. And you're *my* friends.' She said it with a touch of defensiveness and Ben relented. A suite would be nice and Arianna had clearly broken her own rule about expecting no special treatment because of who her father was.

'It's great. Thank you.'

The matter was closed. Arianna went into the house, returning with a backgammon set, and he made coffee, taking the two cups out onto the veranda.

It all felt so natural. So unremarkable, and yet so very delicious. Drinking coffee and playing backgammon to the sound of the sea. Watching Arianna's face as she pondered her next move.

He *had* to be here for her. He'd been there on the ferry, and swum with her away from the treacherous undertow that threatened to pull them both down. Now she needed him again. Ben had never had the chance to go back and save Emma, and saving Arianna now seemed all the more important because of that.

But he mustn't get too involved. She needed to find her own way, and Ben's instinct to overprotect the people he loved would only hinder her. It was a fine line, made all the more difficult by the attraction he felt for Arianna. But this was an opportunity he'd never have again.

Before it was time to think about heading down to the harbour to catch the last ferry, Arianna had already begun to yawn. That was exactly what Ben had planned on.

'I should be going. Lizzie wants to leave early tomorrow morning and we'll be on the eight o'clock ferry, so I need to repack everything tonight.'

Arianna got to her feet. 'I'll give you a lift.'

'No, I'll walk.' Arianna opened her mouth to protest and he silenced her with a stern look. 'You think I went to all this trouble just so you could wake yourself up again by driving?'

She thought for a moment, and Ben hoped

that she was seeing sense. 'I do feel a bit tired. Would you like to take my car? You can leave it at the harbour and then use it to drive to the hotel in the morning. Then bring it back here.'

'I'm coming back in the morning?' Ben teased her, knowing full well that he couldn't keep away. If Arianna wanted him around, he'd be there for her.

'Are you?' She called his bluff and Ben gave in.

'I'll be back. What time tomorrow?'

He was expecting her to just wave her hand, in the way that many people here seemed to do when time was referred to, but Arianna seemed to want something more precise.

'About ten? Or later if you have things to do.'

Ben wondered if she'd be counting the moments, the way he already was. 'Ten's fine. See you then.'

She dropped her car keys into his hand, and followed him outside. As he drove away he saw her standing in the light from the open front door.

Ben had been careful to curb his expectations when he'd come to Ilaria. He hadn't taken it for granted that they'd be friends, or that she'd even want to see him again. But what he'd found here was beyond anything he could have imagined. They'd just clicked together like two pieces of a jigsaw puzzle.

Being there for her was a challenge, one he wasn't sure he was equal to. But everything depended on getting this right. It was his second chance. The one he'd thought he'd never have to be the man that he wanted to be, and if he let Arianna down now that man would be lost for ever.

Last night, Arianna had watched Ben drive away and then walked, yawning, to her bedroom. She'd gone to sleep, curled up with her memories of him, and then woken again at three in the morning, taunted by her nightmares. Wrapping a quilt around her, she'd gone outside to sit on the veranda. The sun had risen, and she'd had breakfast. And the last thought she'd had was that she must take a shower and get dressed…

Now she was being woken by the brush of fingers against her hand. Nice. She shifted a little on the wide settle, then stretched, and *then* realised that the touch was real and not part of a dream.

'Hey...sorry, I didn't mean to startle you.' Ben pulled back, taking Jonas with him. The boy was staring at her, tilting his head to one side in curiosity.

'Hi, Jonas... Ben...' Arianna rubbed her eyes. 'Sorry, is it ten o' clock already...?'

'Just gone. We paced up and down outside your front door a bit before we decided to come around to the back to see if we could find you.'

Arianna chuckled. 'Don't bother about the pacing. Turning up at my back door and giving me a shake is just fine.' Although Ben's gentle touch had been fine too. A lot better than fine, and Arianna hoped that her half-awake face hadn't betrayed her pleasure.

'Did you sleep last night?'

The opportunity to say that she'd had eight solid hours and that she was feeling entirely rejuvenated and ready to start the day was gone. 'I went to bed straight after you left. Slept through till about three.'

He nodded. 'That's something. You want coffee?'

'Yes. Please.' Arianna remembered that the oversized T-shirt she was wearing didn't cover her legs, and wrapped the quilt around her body, getting to her feet. 'I'll be back in a moment.'

'Take your time.' Jonas seemed about to follow Arianna indoors, and Ben caught his hand firmly. 'Come and help me, Jonas.'

Clearly coffee-making wasn't as interesting to Jonas as following Arianna into her bedroom, but Jonas reluctantly went with his father. Ben didn't look back, and Arianna decided not to either.

When she arrived back on the veranda she felt a little more awake and rather more embarrassed about being caught napping. Ben said nothing, though, putting two cups of freshly brewed coffee down on the table, along with a jug of iced lemonade and some glasses. Jonas had been sitting on the steps, which led down from the veranda and onto the beach, but when he saw her he jumped up and flung his arms around her waist.

'Are you ill?' He looked up at her and Arianna smiled.

'No, sweetie, I'm not ill. Just a bit tired. Your dad's made me coffee and that'll wake me up.'

Jonas frowned. 'Dad says that *I* have to get a good night's sleep. I'm not allowed coffee.'

Ben flashed her a get-out-of-that-one smile and sat down at the table.

'Dad's right. We'll both make sure we do that, shall we?'

Jonas nodded, seemingly happy with the answer. Arianna sat down opposite Ben, picking up the small coffee cup and draining half of it in one swallow.

'Glad *I'm* allowed coffee.' She leaned forward, murmuring quietly, and Ben chuckled.

'You're not off the hook, though. Sleep's better.'

'Yes, Dad,' Arianna teased him, and he shrugged, pulling a resigned face. 'How's the hotel?'

'It's great. Lizzie loves it and she asked me to thank you for the fruit basket.'

Arianna nodded. 'My pleasure. So what

would you like to do today? We have a whole island, and I'll be your tour guide.'

Ben had been just about to gently put his real purpose here today to Arianna. Maybe casually and a little obliquely, a friendly reminder that a relaxing day might help her deal with her nightmares. Jonas put a spoke in the wheel of his plans.

'Dad says that we're going to look after you.' He frowned, obviously trying to reconcile an inconsistency. 'Even if you aren't ill.'

Her eyebrows shot up. 'Really?'

In for a penny, in for a pound. Now that Jonas had introduced this new approach, he had little choice but to go with it.

'Yes, really. You're tired and your nightmares are beginning to take over. You need to do something Arianna; they won't go away all on their own.'

'Yes!' Jonas chimed in. 'I don't like nightmares. Dad has to grab the monsters and throw them out of the window.' He illustrated his point by acting out the grabbing of a monster and its disposal out of an imaginary window.

'You can do that?' She looked up at Ben, her gaze softening suddenly.

'Yeah. We…um… Sometimes they wriggle a bit and we have to fight them first.'

'Dad rolls around on the carpet, wrestling them. But he always wins.' Jonas threw himself down onto the ground in a life and death struggle with an imaginary monster. 'Monsters don't like it if you fight them; they get scared.'

Arianna was laughing now, but he could see understanding in her eyes. Maybe the monsters that she faced weren't so different from the ones that occasionally inhabited any child's dreams, even if they were much more persistent.

'That would be very nice. So we're going to practise fighting monsters?'

Jonas was nodding his head vigorously, and Ben stepped in before he could invite Arianna to show him her best fighting moves.

'I just thought that a relaxing day might give you a more restful night.' Ben wasn't entirely sure that relaxation was all Arianna needed. Talking about it, voicing the terrors that dogged her seemed to be a more necessary part of the process. Maybe a day spent doing nothing much at all would encourage her to do that.

She slipped out of her seat to bend down in front of Jonas. 'What do you say to making another sandcastle? A bigger one than last time.'

'Yes!' Jonas nodded vigorously and Arianna got to her feet, smiling.

'Looks as if that's today planned out, then.'

Ben had applied all of his ingenuity to the new sandcastle. He'd made a central lake this time and while Arianna and Jonas sculpted a sand cliff that ran up to the level of the veranda, he had constructed an arrangement of beakers and straws, taped together to make a water cascade, which syphoned water over the edge of the veranda in a small waterfall, to fill the lake.

Jonas was so happy with it all. Ben was a great dad, and his own pleasure in playing with his son was obvious. Arianna dimly remembered her own father playing with her and Xander, but then his grief had taken him away from her. Even now, it felt wrong that she should resent that, when her parents had suffered so much at the loss of their son.

Enjoying this didn't feel quite right either. Xander had never had the chance to play again, or to grow up and play with his own children. Arianna got to her feet, brushing sand from her dress and leaving Jonas and Ben to get on with their castle. The wide settle on the veranda was somewhere to sit and watch, without being a part of it all. Here she felt less like a thief, stealing sandcastles from her brother.

When Ben joined her on the veranda they sat together in silence for a while, watching Jonas. Arianna poured two glasses of lemonade from the jug, pushing one towards Ben.

'I was wondering…' She felt so close to him when they talked, but right now she didn't want to think about her own life. Arianna wanted to know more about his.

'Yeah?'

'What did you mean about the day on the ferry changing your life too? I know how it changed mine, but surely what you did couldn't have given you any regrets.'

He took a swig from his glass. 'No regrets.

Just an impossible set of aspirations for me to live up to.'

'How so?'

Ben shook his head. 'You don't want to hear about that.'

'Why not? It strikes me that it changed us both, and that maybe we're two sides of a coin. Maybe it only really makes sense if we can see both sides.'

He thought it over carefully, and then nodded. 'It was an odd experience for me. I was so elated, and then there was…nothing. I got to the shore and found my mum and dad— all they were worried about was that I was safe, and I didn't tell them about you because I knew they'd tell me off for jumping in after you. You were my secret.'

'A good one?' Arianna rather liked the idea.

'Yeah, you were a great secret to have. It felt as if I was a superhero and I could dress up at night and climb out of the window and do things that no one else could do.'

'Did you?'

'I thought a lot about it. I couldn't get a handle on the logistics of how I was going to make my way down from the first-floor window of a suburban semi without breaking my neck, so I decided to leave it awhile until I had my own place. Somewhere to hang my superhero costume where my mum wouldn't find it when she was tidying up.'

'So you went to medical school. Super doc.'

Ben chuckled. 'There was an element of that. I just knew that there was someone in the world who might have drowned without me. It made me feel good that you must be out there somewhere, leading your life the way you were meant to. When I think about it, it was probably quite convenient that I didn't know you. Always best to keep the objects of those kinds of daydreams one-dimensional.'

He wasn't quite making a joke of all this, but he was keeping it light. Somewhere beneath all that there was pain. Arianna nodded, smiling, and waited for Ben to guide her towards that pain. Maybe if they shared their pain then it would make sense to both of them.

'Being a doctor went some way towards injecting a dose of reality. There are things we can't do, but there are also ways that we *can* make a difference. It meant a lot to me that I was able to help people.'

Arianna nodded. 'It means a lot to me too. Surely that hasn't changed for you?'

It had. She could see it from the flash of guilt and regret in his face. He glanced over towards his son, who was busy landscaping his new castle, completely unaware of their conversation.

'When Emma died…things weren't going so well for us. I can't help wondering if her last thought was that I'd let her down.'

Arianna knew full well that guilt had a big part in grief. All the things that could never be changed, never be taken back.

'What do you mean?'

'I wasn't living at home when Emma died. We'd been arguing a lot, and we were both tired. I told her that I loved her, and suggested that we take a couple of weeks out, so we could reconnect with the things that really mattered. I'm not sure she completely understood.'

'I'm so sorry, Ben. Surely you can't think that you let her down, though. From what you say, you were trying to save your marriage.'

'I was. We both were, and I know we would have succeeded, given a bit of time. I just wonder whether she knew how much I loved her and Jonas.' Ben took a deep breath, his face suddenly haggard.

'In my experience—' Arianna puffed out a breath '—not that I have a great deal of experience in making relationships work, but I think you always do know when someone honestly loves you.'

'Maybe. I hope you're right.' He turned his gaze up to meet hers and something in his eyes made Arianna dread whatever he was about to say next.

'When the accident happened, Emma was on her way to do the weekly shop. A lorry swerved to avoid something and skidded out of control. Witnesses said that it was coming towards the passenger side of the car, where Jonas was in the car seat at the back. Emma couldn't avoid it, but she turned the wheel so that it hit her side of the car.'

'Ben, I...' Arianna shook her head. 'That was a very brave and loving thing to do.'

'She was like that. She could be fierce at times, and we used to argue but... I just hope she knew that I would have done anything to be sitting in the driver's seat, so that Emma and Jonas would have been safe on the other side of the car. If there was any way that I could go back...'

'I believe you.' Arianna almost choked on the words. What *she* believed probably meant less than nothing to Ben. But his face softened suddenly, and he nodded.

'Thank you.' Ben reached across the table, covering her hands with his. 'If I'm honest, this is one of the reasons I came here. Those superhero dreams I had when I was a kid were more precious to me than I knew. Since Emma died, I've lost the feeling that I can make a difference to anyone and... I miss it.'

He'd saved *her*. That might not be very important to him, and it might not be so important to her father, who yearned for his lost son. It meant a lot to Arianna, though.

'Thank you for saving me. I know it's not much of a consolation...'

Ben gave her hands a squeeze and then let go of them. 'It's means more to me than you know. But today wasn't supposed to be about making *me* feel better.'

'As I said. Two sides of one coin. It feels as if we both started from the same place.'

He nodded, clearly turning the idea over in his head. 'Maybe you're right...'

'I think that Jonas knows his dad is a superhero, who protects him against monsters. Kids are pretty switched on about that kind of thing and maybe you should listen to him.'

There was no opportunity for Ben to think about it and decide. Suddenly he was on his feet. 'Jonas, what are you doing? You'll hurt yourself.'

Jonas was upside down in a heap on the sand, and turned himself back up the right way, looking a little shamefaced. 'I want to do somersaults.'

'Not like that, mate.'

'Auntie Lizzie showed Callie how to do one. I want to do them too—show *me*.'

Ben rolled his eyes and then turned back to his son, taking the steps down from the veranda two at a time. 'I can't do a somersault either. And Callie's a bit older than you—that's probably why Auntie Lizzie showed her, don't you think?'

Jonas's face began to crease. 'But, Dad...'

Arianna ventured to the top of the steps. If Ben could come to terms with the past, then so could she. She could do nothing about all the things that Xander had missed out on, but there was one thing she could do for Jonas.

'I can do somersaults...'

Two sets of blue eyes suddenly turned in Arianna's direction. She couldn't resist those eyes, not the father's nor the son's. Ben smiled, heat igniting in his gaze, and then turned to Jonas.

'Perhaps Arianna can show you how to do a somersault?'

Jonas cheered up immediately. 'Yes! Show me!'

CHAPTER SEVEN

BEN HAD WATCHED Arianna on the beach. Her sleeveless T-shirt and shorts accentuated the slim, rounded curves of her figure, and the near-perfect somersaults accentuated its strength. He'd come here with the idea that maybe he could get back in touch with a part of himself that was dying, and which he knew he needed, not just for Jonas but for his patients as well. He'd found a woman who was vulnerable and trying in her own way to deal with the fallout from that day on the ferry, and now it occurred to him that maybe Arianna was right. Maybe they were two sides of a coin, and they could save each other.

Despite all of her protests, he made lunch. Arianna knew what that meant. He was here for her, and he wanted to lift the weight from her shoulders a little so that she could take some time to deal with the grief that had been waiting for her for so long. Her smile and murmured acknowledgement told him that she appreciated the gesture.

They ate, another long, lazy meal. As the sun climbed in the sky and the heat became oppressive, Arianna asked him how Jonas might feel about a siesta.

'I think he could do with one.' Jonas was looking a little heavy-eyed now, after a full morning and a good lunch. 'I was up pretty late last night; I could too.'

She nodded, ushering him and Jonas into a spare bedroom with white walls and a match-ing white bedspread. It looked cool and calm, and when she opened the windows and door he could hear the relaxing roll of the waves.

Jonas was half asleep already. Ben stripped off his beach shoes and T-shirt and laid him down on the bed, sitting down in the arm-chair in the corner of the room and watching his son. He'd promised himself that Jonas was all he'd ever want, all he'd ever need and that he'd always be there to protect him. But the lifelong connection with Arianna was stron-ger than he'd thought, and he wanted to pro-tect her too.

The long net curtains billowed lazily in the

breeze, as if cool and calm was something you could see as well as feel. The house was silent, and Ben's eyes began to droop. Maybe Arianna would be getting some much-needed sleep as well.

A sound, carrying through the silence, and his eyes flipped open. Another, which sounded like a strangled sob, and he was on his feet. Arianna's bedroom door was open, to take advantage of the breeze, and he could see her, sitting up straight in her bed, a light cover clutched around her body.

'Arianna…' His voice was a hoarse whisper and she didn't react. Maybe he should go…

And leave her to her dreams? The swirling water, closing over her head? Ben stepped into the room, sitting down on the edge of the bed.

'Arianna.' He spoke again, and this time he heard his own strength, seeping into his tone.

'It's…just a dream…' Her breathing was ragged and her shaking hands moved to cover her face.

'I know.' He moved closer, wrapping his arm around her shoulders. She nestled against him, clinging to him.

'I'm okay. I'm so tired, Ben. I'll go back to sleep now.'

No, she wouldn't. She'd lie here, wide-eyed, as the cool silence provided a backdrop to a terrifying world. In two hours she'd shower and emerge from her bedroom and down another cup of coffee, to banish her sleeping hours and let the day take over again. That wasn't how she could find healing, and Arianna knew that as well as he did.

'Lie down.' He wrapped the bedspread around her and laid her down on the bed. Shifting across, he propped one leg up on the bed, in a sign that he wasn't going anywhere until she was asleep again. 'Is that okay?'

She reached for him, pulling him down next to her. Then she curled her body against his. 'That's better.'

He dared to put his arm around her, and she laid her head on his shoulder. Despite the fact that Jonas was asleep next door and Arianna needed his comfort, it was still electrifying. It had been so long since he'd felt passion, and it made Ben's head swim a little.

He knew he should pull away from her, but he couldn't help it. When he drew her close she snuggled against him. Arousal gave way to a much more potent emotion. Arianna trusted him to quiet her fears, and somewhere inside he felt the stirring of a determination not to let her down.

He lay still, helpless in the face of Arianna's bravery and her determination to keep going, however much she was hurting inside. Unable to defend himself against the feeling that this was exactly where he should be.

'Tell me about your dream.'

'It doesn't matter.'

'Really? You're going to go with that, are you?'

'You're going to fight my monsters? And throw them out of the window?'

'If that's what it takes.'

He felt her heave a sigh. 'It was… Usually I dream about the ferry. About falling off and you coming to get me, and then watching you get pulled away by the tide. This time… I dreamt I was under the water and you didn't come and get me. There was something pulling me down… Trying to drown me.' She was nearing the part that was most disturbing to her.

'What pulled you down?'

'It was Xander. His face was all puffy, as if he'd been in the water for days.' She looked up at him, her face silhouetted against the pillow. 'Why would I dream that, Ben? Xander was my brother, and he wouldn't do anything like that to me. He loved me…'

'You're the one best able to make sense of your own dreams. But maybe it's your own memories of what happened to your brother on that day that are pulling you down.'

'What do you mean?'

'It's just that…you told me that you felt guilty about your brother's death.' Ben ventured the thought as gently as he could.

He felt her whole body stiffen against his, a sure sign that he was getting close to an awful truth that she didn't want to recognise. 'Guilt wouldn't be logical. I was only six years old.'

She felt it, though. He could hear it in her voice. 'Kids have a habit of feeling that the world revolves around them. That they can control things that even adults can't.'

He felt her sigh. Maybe she was in the same world that he was at the moment—two kids in the water, trying to swim to safety. Holding onto each other as tight as they could.

'If you get the dream again, could you tell yourself what you've just told me? That you were six years old, and it wasn't your fault.'

'I don't know. I could try…' She snuggled against him, slipping her hand into his, and Ben held her close. That same fire, the determination to change her world, was licking around him. He hadn't lost it for good.

'Close your eyes. I'll be here.' That was all she needed to know. He couldn't be here for ever; he had to go home in less than three weeks. Ben hoped that would be enough for both of them.

Arianna had suggested they drive down to the harbour, so that Ben and Jonas could take a look around. She knew everyone and Jonas was made a particular fuss of, being invited to taste slices of succulent fruit and small, sweet baked delicacies in the shops they visited. Ben's presence on Kantos yesterday had already spread to Ilaria and he recognised the Greek word for *doctor* when Arianna introduced him to people. Clearly she wasn't about to tell anyone that they'd met on the ferry, and that was fine by Ben. It had been their secret for so long now that it seemed only right it should remain so a little longer.

They dined at the taverna, their table moving steadily across the floor as people that Arianna knew arrived with their families and friends, and tables were pushed together. By the time the meal had been finished, two hours later, they were sitting with twenty other people, and those who could speak English were vying to translate the jokes that flew across the table for Ben.

When they left, obviously a little early by local standards as there were still children of Jonas's age sitting at the table, Arianna worked her way around the table, saying her goodbyes. Ben was required to do the same, and Jonas followed suit as well. Then they took the coast road, driving around the island to their hotel, bright stars above their heads, the moon reflecting in the dark sea to one side.

'Thank you. We've had a great day.'

Jonas had fallen asleep in the car, and Ben carried him in his arms to the entrance. The foyer was still bustling with activity and even a friendly kiss goodnight seemed too much. It might have started out as something brushed onto her cheek, but the temptation of her lips was far too great.

'Thank *you*, Ben. For everything.' Arianna deposited a kiss on the ends of her fingers and pressed it to Jonas's sleeping brow. It was the perfect way out of the dilemma, and accompanied by a flash of fire in her warm eyes.

'You'll be all right? Tonight…?' Suddenly he couldn't bear to leave her, alone in the darkness, prey to all the terrors that the night brought her.

'I'll be fine.' Arianna said the words a little too quickly, and Ben guessed they were her stock response to any enquiry about her own well-being. 'I sleep on my own every night.'

But tonight… Ben discarded the thought. His role in her life was already a complex mixture of checks and balances. Talking with her and sharing his own feelings, and listening to hers. Being there for her, but not getting so close that his protectiveness became challenging.

'Would you like to go up to the Lava Lake tomorrow?' She seemed determined to leave him on a positive note, and Ben should take a leaf from her book.

'I don't want to impose.' Maybe she had things to do. People to see.

'You're not. I love the Lava Lake and I haven't been up there for ages. This is a great excuse for me to go.'

It didn't take much to convince him. 'In that case, thank you. We'd love it.'

'I'll pick you up at ten? I'll bring lunch.'

'Ten's great. Any time—we'll go to the pool and if you want to sleep late…' Ben probably shouldn't mention that, since Arianna was clearly skating around the subject.

'Okay. I'll meet you there. Ten o'clock, Greek time. That's any time before noon, English time.'

She turned and walked to her car, waving to him before she got in. As Ben watched her go, the entirely honourable impulse to save her from her nightmares vied with a slightly less honourable yearning to just hold her close while she slept. He turned away, walking into the hotel building and telling himself that both were unacceptable. He hadn't been there for Emma, and he couldn't promise to be there for anyone else now.

Arianna arrived at the pool at ten thirty the following morning, clearly in no rush to get started because she sat down in the chair next to Ben's and when he offered her a drink she accepted it readily, choosing a cocktail of different fruit juices from the bar menu.

'You've brought your bathing suits with you?' she asked, almost as an afterthought, as they walked down to the dock, and Ben nodded. He'd heard that swimming at the Lava Lake was an experience not to be missed.

She had a child-sized life jacket for Jonas, and made sure that it was fitted correctly, before starting the engine of the boat and speeding towards Kantos. She made a circuit of the island, so that Jonas could see it all from the sea, and then slipped into a secluded inlet to moor the boat. Putting on a wide-brimmed sunhat with a blue ribbon that matched her dress, Arianna caught up her straw bag, looping it over her shoulder, before leading them along a gently sloping path.

'How are you doing?' The path had become steep and rocky, and Jonas looked as if he was getting tired. 'You want a lift for this last bit?'

Jonas nodded, and while he was lifting the boy onto his back, Arianna picked up the bag that contained their towels and swimming trunks and they toiled their way up the hill.

'It's worth it when we get there.'

'Yep.' Jonas seemed to be getting both taller and heavier by the hour, these days. And his excited wriggling wasn't helping much either.

'Wait and see…' Arianna seemed to be walking faster instead of slower now and Ben lengthened his stride to keep up with her.

'Woah, Dad!' They got to the brow of the hill and a picture-perfect view revealed itself. The water was the deepest blue he'd ever seen, and the large lake was surrounded by steep slopes, some of them sparkling in the sunshine from the seams of crystalline rock formed by the intense heat of a long-dormant volcano.

'What do you think?' Arianna was looking up at him with shining eyes.

'Spectacular. Far better than I'd expected.'

They slithered down the steep slope to the water's edge, Ben keeping a tight hold on Jonas's hand and reaching for Arianna's when it looked as if she might lose her balance. When she took it, she held on tight.

Jonas ran down to the water's edge, picking up a shiny blue stone. 'Look, Dad. I'm going to take it home.'

Ben shook his head. 'No, we leave everything as we find it. The next person won't be able to see that stone if you take it away with you. You can take some pictures, though, if you want.'

He pulled his phone out of his pocket and gave it to Jonas, who dropped the stone and started taking pictures.

'It doesn't matter,' Arianna murmured, pointing to a glistening blue cliff on the other side of the lake. 'There's plenty left. That's where they've taken little pieces of stone off for the souvenir shops. They're only allowed to take so much, but taking a little has uncovered what's been hidden by shale and vegetation.'

'It's the principle. He's happy taking photographs.'

When Jonas had finished taking photographs of different shaped stones, he decided that he wanted a few selfies. He posed for a while, and then tired of that. Arianna took the phone from his hand, holding it out and taking a shot of the two of them, and then Ben was dragged away from the view to join them. He felt her curls brush his cheek as he leaned in close. Just like a happy family.

He shouldn't think like that. But when he held the phone out to get a shot of the three of them, with the lake as a backdrop, he couldn't help it. He took another shot of Arianna and Jonas, standing at the water's edge, and then managed to capture Arianna in a perfect star jump, her dress flapping around her legs in the breeze. Ben wondered if he'd ever tire of this, but finally Arianna called a halt.

'Shall we rest a while? Then we can go swimming.'

'Sounds good.' Resting generally meant food and a lazy siesta, and this time was no different. Arianna found a grassy spot, shaded by trees that grew almost horizontally out of the sides of the slope, spread out a light quilted groundsheet and proceeded to unpack plastic tubs of food from her bag. Ben took three bottles of water from his bag, and they sat down to eat. Bread to dip into the tubs of tzatziki and hummus, with salads and chicken on paper plates.

When Arianna had collected up the remains of the meal, Jonas curled up beside her, ready to take a siesta now. Ben watched as she lay down beside his son, her arm thrown protectively across Jonas's chest.

This was his for the day, with photographs to remember it by. The pretence of a happy family, just like the one that he'd allowed to slip through his fingers. It might not be his to take, but he could allow himself to enjoy the feeling for a little while.

Ben had been watching over her as she slept. She'd seen him, through heavy-lidded eyes, as she'd dozed, and the knowledge that he was there had chased away her dreams.

He was right. This weekend had been harder than any other, but she was finally facing the feelings she'd been bottling up for years. If Ben hadn't been here she would have retreated into her work again, and pushed them all aside, but now they were bubbling to the surface like a volcano, threatening to explode.

When Jonas began to stir against her, Ben was still leaning on his elbows, still there. Arianna climbed across the rocks, finding a place where she could change into her bathing suit, and then raced down to the water's edge. Ben and Jonas were already there, trying to get each other as wet as possible in as short a time as possible.

The man had everything. Physique, tone, good looks. His blond hair and pale skin were almost golden in the sunshine, and the rivulets of water running down his chest... She just couldn't look. If she looked, then she'd stare.

'It's very quiet here,' Ben remarked as they both bobbed lazily in the water, while Jonas splashed around, doggy-paddling backwards and forwards, never more than an arm's length away from his father.

'Yes. It's not that easy to get to. Although soon there will be more tourists on Kantos. There's a new hotel being built this year; they've already laid the foundations.'

'Yeah? Is that good or bad?'

'It gives me a bit of a problem. It'll mean that I can't cover both islands properly, so I'm going to have to take on another doctor at the health centre.'

'It won't be difficult to find someone, will it. Who's going to turn down the chance to work here?'

Arianna chuckled. It was nice that he thought that this was the kind of place that anyone would want to be. 'A lot of doctors prefer to work in the city. Getting someone to come here for six months or a year isn't too hard, but getting someone who'll stay can be a challenge.'

'I'm sure you'll get the right person. Will the hotel change things here on the island? How do local people feel about it?'

'They're all for it; it brings money here and provides people with jobs. It's going to be away from the village, much like the one on Ilaria. And it'll be low-rise and sympathetic to the local style of construction.'

'Your father's building it?'

'Yes, he is.'

'He seems to have a monopoly on hotels

in this area…' Ben broke off, shooting her a querying glance as Arianna quirked the corners of her mouth down. 'Is that a problem?'

'No, what my father's doing in these islands is great; he's developing in a way that supports local communities rather than overwhelming them…' Arianna let out a sigh. 'But I've worked pretty hard to make a place for myself here. I want people to see me for what I am, not what my father can buy.'

'You can't buy your way through seven years of medical training.'

Money obviously didn't impress Ben; he had a different idea about the things that mattered. He valued the same things that she did, and it occurred to Arianna that their ambitions had been forged in the same place and at the same time, in the swirling waters around the sinking ferry.

'Some people think you can. They think that having everything materially means that you have everything you need.'

'Yeah, I suppose so. I was lucky, growing up. We had *enough* in terms of material things and everything we needed. My dad's an academic, and there's a great deal of satisfaction in the job for him, but not a massive amount of money.'

'That sounds nice. Does he teach?' Arianna could imagine Ben's father as a teacher. Ben had that way about him, of listening to what people said and nurturing a conversation.

'Yeah, he's a university professor and he teaches Ancient History. That's what we were doing in Greece; he'd come to meet up with some of his contacts in the museums in Athens. Ilaria was my mum's idea; she wanted to get out of the city and spend some time on the beach.'

'Grandad's going to build me a…what is it?' Jonas had obviously been half listening to their conversation and his ears had pricked up at the mention of his grandfather.

'A trireme.' Ben grinned at his son. 'A model of a trireme, that is, not a full-sized one.'

'No. We don't have room.' Jonas started swimming again, his flailing arms and legs seeming to expend the maximum amount of energy for the minimum amount of progress.

'Try holding onto me if you want to stay in

one place, Jonas. Like you do in your swimming class.'

'I can do it, Dad. I don't need to hold on.'

'Yeah, okay. As long as you're managing.' Ben rolled his eyes, and left his son to it. 'Don't let us stop you if you want to go for a swim, Arianna. We'll just stay here and do some pretend swimming.'

'I can do proper swimming.' Jonas's body straightened in the water suddenly and he swam a couple of yards in a very respectable front crawl, before reverting back to doggy-paddle. 'I like this better.'

'Okay. I wouldn't want Arianna to think that I hadn't taught you how to swim properly when you want to.'

'If you like, I can look after Jonas for a little while. You can't come to the Lava Lake without swimming out to the middle and just ducking your head under the water.' Arianna gestured towards the centre of the lake.

'Why, what's there?'

'You have to see for yourself.' She wanted Ben to remember today, and it was difficult to forget swimming in the water above the blue-green crystals that had formed at the deepest point of the bed of the lake.

'You'll be okay here?'

'I won't take my eyes off Jonas for a second.'

Thank you. His lips formed silent words that were only for her, and then Ben spoke to his son. 'Jonas, you'll stay with Arianna, won't you? If she says you're to get out of the water then you get out of the water.'

He waited for Jonas's confirmation that he'd heard and understood and then started to swim towards the middle of the lake. Arianna watched the strong swell of his shoulders, keeping her hand on Jonas's back, ready to grab hold of him if it looked as if he were tiring.

But now that Ben was gone, her fears seemed to swell in her chest. A sudden vision hit her, of Jonas—or was it Xander?—being sucked beneath the surface of the water. She should get a grip, but all she could think about was getting Jonas to the safety of the beach.

'Have you finished swimming now, Jonas?'

The boy was obviously tiring a little but he ignored her, still splashing about.

'Let's get out, shall we?' Arianna tried again.

'Okay.' Jonas swam towards the shore and Arianna heaved a sigh of relief. She felt stupid now, wrapping him in a towel to dry him, and then finding his hat and T-shirt to protect him from the sun. But she did feel a bit more confident.

Ben had reached the middle of the lake and was waving to her. He must be wondering what she was doing, and she waved back. Ben returned her thumbs-up signal, and ducked his head beneath the surface.

Arianna started to count the seconds. She knew exactly what he was seeing right now; she'd swum out and experienced it often enough herself. He was surrounded by iridescent blues, the colours intensifying the deeper he went. Still, she counted. It was tempting to lose yourself down there, and perhaps she should have warned him.

His head broke the surface and he waved again. Arianna cupped her hands around her mouth, shouting across the water, 'Don't stay down too long.'

Stupid. He knew that. He could have stayed and dived again, maybe even for a little longer, but now Ben had turned in the water, and was striking back towards the shore.

He got out of the water, slicking his hair back as he walked towards her. Did he really *have* to do that? Keeping her hands off him was difficult enough…

'You saw it? The bed of the lake?'

'Yes, I did. It's amazing.'

'Don't you want to dive again, and see it a second time?'

He pressed his lips together, puffing out a breath. 'No, once is enough…'

Arianna narrowed her eyes. 'You're the first person I've brought here who's said that.'

He shrugged, bending down to pick up a dry towel and wrapping it around her shoulders. Suddenly he leaned in to give her a hug, and she felt the taut muscle of his arm against her cheek before he drew back again.

'Are you okay?'

Somehow he understood how fearful she'd been. Maybe he'd heard it in the urgency of her tone, when she'd called across the water to him.

'I…wasn't. I am now. I thought I'd be all right on my own with Jonas, but I didn't realise how being in the water with him would make me feel. But you can go back if you want. It would actually make me feel a little better, knowing I haven't spoiled the day.'

He brushed his fingers against her cheek. 'You could never spoil any of my days, Arianna. I'd rather be here if you need me.'

That protective instinct of his again. 'What I really need you to do at the moment is to give me a chance to try again and do it right. We'll be fine, I promise. Jonas has already found something he wants to do.'

Ben looked across to where his son was busy arranging stones into piles, according to their colour. Arianna wondered if he really could bring himself to be a little less vigilant, just this once.

'Fine as in *fine*? Or as in keeping up appearances?'

'Fine as in absolutely fine. And I really want you to go.'

He thought for a moment and then nodded. 'Okay. You'll call me if you want me to come back?'

'I'll call. Don't worry about that.'

Arianna watched as he walked back down

to the water's edge, wading in and then diving forward and starting to swim strongly. Maybe if he wasn't so physically perfect, if she didn't crave his touch as much as she needed his comfort, this would all be a little bit easier. But she and Ben were linked now. Linked by their shared past and the way they seemed to understand each other.

She might as well enjoy it. Arianna sat down, pulling her knees up and propping her chin on them. Even at this distance, there *was* a lot to enjoy.

CHAPTER EIGHT

SHE DROPPED BEN and Jonas off at their hotel. It had been a wonderful day, and seeing Ben and Jonas explore the Lava Lake had given a place that she loved an extra lustre.

Arianna had noticed Ben watching her drive away in her rear-view mirror. He'd done that last night as well, and it produced a mixture of emotions. She didn't want him to fuss, he'd been doing enough of that already, and she'd cope the way she always had. But having him there, to help her cope, was a powerful temptation.

One that she had to resist. The smile that lingered on her face as she drove home would be enough to carry her through until tomorrow. It had to be.

It was still early, and she walked out onto the veranda, listening to the calm rhythm of the sea. It lulled her into a half-asleep doze, too drowsy to go to bed, until her eyes snapped open at the sound of the knock on her front door.

Being the only doctor on the island was a twenty-four-hour-a-day job. Arianna didn't mind that, but it always seemed to be the case that people picked the one hour that she most wanted to herself. She stood up, pasting a smile on her face, which promptly slid to the floor when she opened the door and saw Ben.

Is something the matter? He looked as if everything was right with the world, leaning against one of the pillars that supported the wide porch. His arms were folded and he was smiling in that just-happened-to-be-passing way of his.

He didn't just happen to be anything. He had a child to look after and he'd just walked a couple of miles in the darkness, along the stony path that led directly across the island.

'Where's Jonas?'

'He's in bed. Having a suite makes it easy for Lizzie to keep an eye on him for the night.'

The *whole* night? That sounded challengingly long-term. She supposed the least she could do was to let him in. She stood back from the door, rubbing the sleep out of her eyes.

'I didn't wake you up, did I? All the lights were on.'

What would he have done if they hadn't been? Turned around and walked all the way back? Arianna swallowed the question as it sprang to her lips, not entirely sure that she wanted to hear the answer.

'What's so urgent that it can't wait until the morning, Ben?'

Whatever it was, he seemed determined not to meet her gaze when he said it.

'I…um… I know this weekend has been hard on you, and that my turning up here is one of the things that's caused that. I know that today was difficult in places.'

She couldn't deny what he already knew. 'I have my moments, but they're just moments. I want to just let them go and get on with things.'

This time he could meet her gaze. Perhaps he'd been possessed by the strange spell of the lake, because his eyes seemed even more blue, and more lustrous.

'And you'll let them go tonight? I can't get

into your dreams, Arianna, but maybe I can be there to help.'

Who was he trying to kid? Ben had made his way into her dreams a long time ago, and now he played an almost pivotal role in them. He couldn't quite change their course, the darkness always managed to suck her down, but part of the horror of that was that it was carrying her away from Ben's outstretched hands.

'I have to work things out for myself, Ben. You should be with Jonas.'

He heaved a sigh. 'I went back out to the centre of the lake this afternoon because you told me I should. And you were right. I was being over-protective and you and Jonas didn't need me. How about compromising with me now, and admitting that you might sleep a little better with someone around?'

'With *you* around, you mean?' The words *compromising* and *admitting* grated a little.

'This is not an entirely selfless act. I'm here for me just as much as I am for you. I want to be someone who can make a difference again.'

'I'll be up early in the morning. I have to work tomorrow.'

'Then you'll be needing a good night's sleep beforehand.'

She didn't dare thank him or hug him for being here when she really needed him. Just being one step closer to him would only remind her that she should keep her distance and she'd have to step back again and send him away. Arianna walked to the door of the spare room, opening it wide and stopping it from drifting closed again with an irregularly shaped chunk of granite from the sea that served as both a doorstop and a fascinating piece of nature's art. That was an oblique enough hint that they weren't really sleeping separately, and that her bedroom door would be wide open too.

'I should be turning in now.'

'Yeah. Me too.' Ben held her gaze but didn't move, and Arianna realised that it was because she was standing too close to the doorway. She moved aside to let him into the room.

'Just…help yourself to whatever you need. First one up in the morning makes coffee.'

Arianna had no doubt that the first one awake would be her. These days, she had so little need of her alarm clock that she might as well throw it into the sea.

'It's a deal.' He turned towards the bed and then changed his mind, as if going anywhere near it when she was in his line of sight was a faux pas. 'I'll see you in the morning. Goodnight.'

'Goodnight, Ben. And…thank you for coming over.' Arianna turned, making for her own bedroom.

Ben had taken a risk, but he'd had to come. He'd spoken to Lizzie, who had told him that if he had things to work out with Arianna then he should go. So he'd kissed Jonas goodnight, waited until he was asleep and left.

He'd faced his own diffidence about whether he was really the one to help Arianna and decided that just because he wasn't in the business of saving anyone any more, it didn't mean he couldn't do something. Then he'd faced Arianna. And now he expected himself to just go to sleep?

He slipped off his shoes, and left his chinos and T-shirt laid out so that he could dive back into them at a moment's notice. Lying down on the bed under a crisp white sheet, he stared in the approximate direction of the ceiling. Nights here were darker than the ones in London, where a little bit of the yellow glow of streetlights had a habit of filtering through into a room.

Ben could hear Arianna moving around, and rejected the temptation to imagine what she was doing. He wasn't here for that, and it was wrong to even give it head room. The house was silent now and he turned over, focusing on a different area of darkness in the room.

Maybe he'd dozed off, but he didn't think he had. He could hear someone moving around, footsteps and the rustle of fabric, but the noises were quiet and measured. Ben stayed still, listening for any indication that Arianna was in distress and not just getting out of bed to fetch a glass of water.

'May I come in?' Arianna's words were almost a whisper, and if he'd been asleep he would have missed them entirely.

'Of course.'

A faint shadow moved across the room and the bed moved as she sat down on it. Ben reached for her hand, but couldn't find it.

'Come here…' He shifted back on the bed, to give her space.

She inched towards him, and Ben reached out again, his fingers connecting with hers this time. And there was no resistance when he guided her hand. Arianna lay down next to him on the bed, and Ben tucked her against the curve of his own body, putting his arm around her.

'That's nice.' She was wrapped in the light quilt that he'd found her under the other morning, but he could still appreciate the scent of her hair, and the feel of her fingers twisting around his.

'Yeah. Much better.'

He felt her relax, her head on the pillow next to his. Ben listened to every breath, the way he'd sat and listened to Jonas's breathing when he was a baby, and sometimes still did. It began to steady and slow, as if she were falling asleep.

* * *

She was dreaming. Her fingers clutching at nothing and her legs twitching, as if running fast. Ben pulled Arianna a little closer, careful not to wake her. Maybe she'd feel him there in her dream.

Long moments of agonised waiting. She was quiet and still for a few minutes, and then her body began to move against his again, as if the dream had faded and then returned. And then he felt her jump, a small cry escaping her lips.

'What did you dream, Arianna?' Maybe if she told him now, when she was still half-asleep, she could make a little more sense of it.

'I don't… I don't know.' Her movements were more purposeful now, and she seemed about to pull away from him and sit up.

'Just relax a moment. Tell me about your dream.' Pushing her back into a world that obviously terrified her was a risk. But he couldn't save her from it, and the next best thing was to be with her and try to provide some comfort.

'I'm on the ferry, and then I fall into the

water. I'm being dragged down...' Ben could feel her starting to panic, and he found her hand, winding his fingers around hers. 'I'm being dragged down but... I'm telling Xander to let go. I can't help him, and it's not my fault.'

She'd remembered that, at least, and it was reflected in her dream now. 'Can you find me?'

'No...' Her body tensed suddenly. 'No, I couldn't find you, Ben. You weren't there...'

'I'm here, Arianna. Hold on tight.'

Her fingers clutched his almost painfully. And then she began to relax. Ben suspected that this was usually the point at which she got out of bed and went to sit on the veranda. Sitting up all night had the advantage of clearing your head, but it did nothing for your readiness for work in the morning.

'Go back to sleep. I'm right here, and I've got you. You're safe.'

It had been so long since she'd gone to sleep, wrapped in someone's arms. And Lawrence had never made her feel safe, the way that Ben did. She'd never felt that he could find his way into her dreams and help her fight off the monsters that were waiting for her there.

Arianna hadn't dreamed again that night, and she woke to find herself alone. Lighter, somehow, as if she'd shed some of the weight of guilt that the nightmares always brought with them. She'd thrown off the quilt at some point during the night, and she could still feel the warm thrill of the touch of his skin against hers. Maybe *that* had been a dream, but she didn't think so.

She could hear Ben moving around, and the smell of coffee was tempting her awake. Picking up the quilt from the floor, she wrapped it carefully on top of the sleeveless vest she wore and walked out onto the veranda.

'Coffee! Now!'

Ben's head popped through the open kitchen window. 'Wait! It'll be ready in two minutes. Then we'd better get moving, or Jonas will be wondering where I've got to and you'll be late for work.'

Not a word about the dreams. That was because he'd been there and held her, driving them away. Ben had found two pastries in the bread box and he brought them out with the coffee, sitting down next to her on the long settle so they could both look out at a crisp, clear morning.

'What are you and Jonas up to today?' Arianna took a sip of her coffee.

'We'll probably all go to the beach in the morning. Then we'll take a siesta and I thought I might check out the little museum in the village.'

'Go for three o'clock. It's Andreas's day off today; he's been covering at the health centre this weekend. His father runs the museum and when he has a free day Andreas organises trips down to the harbour, and they teach the kids how to fish. Jonas might enjoy that.'

'That sounds great. I'll take Lizzie's three kids as well, so that she and James can have an afternoon to themselves. My dad's a fisherman and he'd be very impressed if all of his grandchildren come back from holiday knowing how to fish. Do you want to do something this evening?'

Arianna had been hoping that Ben would ask. It would be something to look forward to all day.

'Shall we meet up for dinner at the taverna? About eight?'

'Sounds good. Greek time or English time?' He grinned at her.

'Doctor's time. I'll give you a call if I can't make it.'

That evening Arianna declined the invitations from other diners to join them and they sat alone, under the fairy lights that illuminated the canopy over their heads.

'How was your day?' Ben asked, after Jonas had finished recounting his fishing adventures with his cousins and his new friend Andreas.

'Busy. I was at the hotel this afternoon, but you'd already left to go down to the village.'

'Lizzie said that the manager called her to ask about the children's MMR vaccinations. Was that anything to do with your visit?'

'Yes. There's a case of measles in the hotel, a little girl from England.' Arianna quirked her lips down. 'The parents gave me a bit of a hard time, actually.'

'How so?'

'Well, they insisted that she couldn't have

picked it up in England and that she must have got it here in Greece. They're asking the hotel for compensation.'

'What? How long's she been here?'

'Ten days.' Arianna knew what he was thinking, but the incubation period for measles was between ten and fourteen days. 'She could have picked it up at home, or on the plane, or here. I doubt very much it's here because I haven't had any other cases on the island.'

'Could have been anywhere. What about the other kids at the hotel?'

'I asked the manager to make a list of those who haven't been vaccinated, and I'll be going back tomorrow to see if they have any symptoms. Meanwhile, they've moved the family to one of the separate bungalows in the grounds where they can isolate more comfortably, and deep cleaned their old room.'

Ben nodded. 'That's pretty decent of them. Did you point out to the parents that if they'd had their child vaccinated then she might not have gotten measles in the first place? It's hardly the hotel's fault.'

'That's the thing. I can't really say anything

because everyone knows that my father owns the hotel. I can be as even-handed as I like, but that doesn't stop anyone from accusing me of trying to get the hotel off the hook. Andreas is coming with me tomorrow, but he's not exactly impartial either. His wife works as an accountant at the hotel, and he works at the health centre my father built.'

'What about me? No one can accuse me of being partisan.' Ben looked around, as if daring any of the taverna's patrons to do anything of the kind. 'I'd be happy to go along with you. I may not be able to practise, but as a doctor I do know what I'm seeing and I'm happy to tell anyone who asks.'

It would be the ideal solution. Although there was the small matter of last night... 'You're not exactly an impartial witness, though, are you?'

He heaved a sigh. 'We're friends, Arianna. We've spent time together, and that's no one's business but our own. I'm a doctor, and it's perfectly reasonable that I should take an interest in your practice, and be willing to help out in an unofficial capacity if I can.'

It was. Arianna shifted in her seat, feeling

a little guilty all the same. 'I suppose… If you don't mind.'

'Of course not. I'll ask Lizzie to keep an eye on Jonas…'

'Dad…' Jonas lost interest in the food on his plate suddenly, and looked up at his father. 'Auntie Lizzie just wants to sit on the beach and read her book.'

'You don't like the beach?'

'I like Arianna's beach. And fishing…' Jonas shot his father an imploring look, and Arianna saw the side of Ben's jaw tighten. For a man as tender-hearted as he was, Jonas's pleading looks had to be difficult to bear. Especially when he was being torn in two directions.

'I've got a better idea.' She nudged his elbow. 'Are you happy for me to organise something with Andreas?' Both Ben and Jonas had spent time out fishing with Andreas this afternoon, and Ben would have had the chance to get to know him and see how good he was with children.

'Yes, of course.' Ben didn't hesitate.

Andreas and Eleni were sitting at a table in the far corner of the taverna, and when Arianna explained what was needed they agreed immediately. They hadn't started eating yet, and they brought their drinks over to where Ben and Jonas were sitting. Ben fetched a chair for Eleni and Arianna shifted up a bit so that they could sit down.

'Hey, Jonas.' Andreas grinned at the boy and Jonas's eyes lit up immediately when he saw his new friend.

'Andreas has a few hours off work tomorrow. We thought we might go out fishing,' Eleni added.

'Can I come?'

Eleni smiled at Ben. 'We'd like you to come, but you'll have to ask your dad whether it's all right.'

'Dad, *please…*'

Arianna supposed that Ben might have pretended to think about it, but he was already trying not to laugh. 'Of course you can go, Jonas. Thank you both.'

Andreas smirked. 'Thank *you* for getting me out of going to the hotel tomorrow with Arianna. I'd far rather be fishing.'

The five of them ate together, and then Andreas and Eleni bade them goodnight, telling

Jonas that he was to be ready at three for their fishing expedition. She strolled to her car with Ben, resisting the temptation to slip her hand into the crook of his arm. The time she had left to ask the question that had been nagging at her all evening was dwindling now.

She wanted the sense of security that only Ben could give her. She knew he wouldn't say no if she asked, but somehow she couldn't quite find the words. Jonas was dozing in the back of the car by the time they reached the hotel, and this was Arianna's last chance. She got out of the driver's seat, catching Ben's gaze.

His eyes always took her breath away. Bright in the sunlight, and now the deepest shade of blue possible in the darkness.

'Would you...um...?'

'Yes. I would.'

'You don't know what I'm about to ask yet,' Arianna reproved him.

'Whatever it is, it's a yes.' His fingers found the side of her jaw, his touch sending shivers down her spine.

'I could...wait for you. Until you've put Jonas to bed and he's asleep.' Arianna would wait in the car. Sitting in the suite with Lizzie and James seemed awkward, and she didn't want to share what she had with Ben right now.

'Go home. I'll walk across.'

'But…'

He leaned in, brushing a kiss against her cheek. 'Go home. I'll be there.'

Arianna had changed into a pair of sweatpants and a T-shirt, and curled up on the wide settle on the veranda. Listening to the sound of the sea, the waves measuring time as she waited for him. Then she saw him, at the other end of the veranda.

His shadowy figure, walking towards her, made her catch her breath. Ben sat down at the other end of the settle, stretching his legs out in front of him. It felt as if he was coming home to her.

'Jonas is asleep?'

He nodded. 'He's very excited about going fishing *again* tomorrow. But he settled down in the end.'

'And Lizzie? What does she think about you disappearing for a second night?'

She heard his quiet laugh in the darkness.

'Lizzie and I have an understanding. I didn't play the concerned older brother when she was first dating, and she doesn't give me the concerned little sister act now. We have our own lives.'

'And this is dating?'

He thought for a moment. 'Not sure. What do you reckon?'

'I'm not sure either. I'll let you know as soon as I do.'

Whatever it was, it was fine for Arianna to move towards him, snuggling up against him. He put his arm around her shoulders and they sat in silence, the hurricane lamp on the table flickering feebly, a small pool of light in the darkness.

'So do you? Date.' Arianna tried to make the question sound casual.

'Nope. I have enough on my hands with a job and a child.' Ben laughed quietly. 'That's my excuse, and I'm sticking to it.'

He could have found the time. Arianna knew other single parents who managed to hold down a job and a relationship. But Ben just didn't want to. He was manacled, by his own feelings of guilt and the feeling that he could never again be the person he'd wanted to be.

'Do you? Date,' he asked.

'I have enough on my hands, building up a practice. That's *my* excuse.'

'And what's the real story? I've told you mine.'

'I was engaged once. It didn't work out.' Even that had lost its sting. Somehow, when Ben was around everything else really didn't matter so much. 'I met him at one of my father's parties in London.'

'One of the suitors he had lined up for you?'

'Yes.' Arianna could laugh about it now. 'It was a bit like speed dating. Fifteen minutes apiece, and then I got whisked off to the next one.'

Ben chuckled. 'Did they have to form an orderly queue?'

'No, nothing like that. My father's secretary used to be there though; she's always at his parties to oversee things and she's ferociously efficient. I dare say she had a carefully disguised plan, that didn't look like a plan at all.'

'They're the worst. If you're going to have a

plan, the least you can do is let everyone else in on it. So how did it feel to have all those guys lined up for your appraisal?'

It had always felt to Arianna that it was the other way round, that she was the one on show. Ben put a different perspective on a lot of things.

'When I met Lawrence the first thing he suggested was that we sneak away somewhere, so that we didn't have to be polite and talk to everyone in the room. I liked that about him immediately. He pinched a bottle of champagne and a couple of glasses and we climbed the railings in the square opposite my father's house. I tore my dress.'

'That sounds *very* romantic.' It was difficult to know whether Ben was teasing her or not. It was just his way—laid-back and without attaching any judgements.

'It seemed so at the time. Lawrence didn't much care about rules; he'd just do whatever seemed right at the time.'

'I can't disagree with that approach to life.'

Arianna dug her fingers into his ribs. 'You're quite different. Lawrence always took the easy way out.'

'Trust me. When Jonas makes his mind up about something, the easy way out seems like a very good option.' Ben chuckled.

'That's different. I've always had night-mares from time to time, and Lawrence just used to tell me to get a grip. He didn't see why I'd want to work as a doctor when I didn't have to. My father didn't much like him, but that was the one thing they *did* see eye to eye about.'

'Because, of course, it's up to them what you do with your life.' There *was* a judge-ment there. In the shadows, she could see that Ben's lip had a definite curl to it.

'It became very clear that Lawrence's ex-pectation of marriage was very different to mine. He wanted to live the life that I'd spent all my time trying to get away from. It was one of those tough break-ups where you argue every day for months and finally it's a relief to get away from each other because you're just so exhausted.'

'I'm sorry. It sounds as if he didn't give you what you needed.'

'Lawrence's opinion was that no one could give me what I needed. Too high-maintenance.' Arianna was inclined to agree on that score. She'd never been able to let go of the repercussions that her brother's death had had on her family, even though she'd tried to hide it. Lawrence's observation had hurt, because she knew that it was true.

Ben shook his head. 'That wasn't for him to say. We all need what we need. That's not high-maintenance; it's just a fact of life. High-maintenance is asking for a load of things we don't really need.'

'Maybe...'

He snorted with disgust. 'Come on, Arianna. We're both doctors. Someone comes to see us saying that their leg hurts and we don't tell them to get a grip. We address the problem.'

'Is that what you're doing? Addressing the problem?' Fear lent a sharpness to her tone. She wanted to be more than just a problem that needed addressing to Ben.

He leaned forward slowly, catching her hand in his and raising it to his lips, his eyes dark and tender. A sudden stab of longing penetrated her heart.

'I care about you as a friend. If you want a

doctor, you should go and make an appointment with someone else.'

'I don't want anyone else, Ben. I want you, as my friend.' She clung onto his hand desperately. 'I shouldn't have said what I did. I'm sorry...'

'You have nothing to be sorry for, Arianna. We don't need to define our relationship. I wouldn't know how to.'

Maybe that was his way of avoiding the sexual tension that always seemed to hover around them. Maybe it was hers too. Arianna stifled a yawn. All she really cared about at the moment was that Ben was here, with her.

'It's going to be a hot night. Do you want to sleep outside?'

Arianna's version of doing anything was always far more delightful than Ben could have expected. To him, sleeping outside was a bundle of hastily assembled bedding and a tent. But she shooed him off the long settle, pulling at a mechanism underneath it to unfold it into a full-sized bed.

She brought bedding out from the house, spreading pillows and light quilts. And then the finishing touch. A thin muslin drape was suspended from a hook in the canopy above them and arranged around the edge of the bed. It took five minutes to turn the outdoor dining area into a sleeping area with a touch of magic.

She pulled back the drape a little, sitting down on the bed and beckoning to him. 'What do you think?'

'It's wonderful.' They were surrounded by the sounds and smells of the outdoors, caressed by a fresh breeze from the sea to keep them cool. But here, in their own bubble, all that Ben could see was Arianna.

She was still suddenly, staring into his eyes. In the dark depths of hers, he saw an exploding warmth of desire.

So close. So very close to tipping over into sweet passion. If they did, they could never go back, but Ben couldn't resist. He dropped a kiss onto his own fingers, brushing it against her mouth.

Arianna smiled, raising her hand to her lips and transferring her own kiss to his mouth in return. The feeling was breathtaking, so much from such a small gesture.

'You are so beautiful.' He took her hand, feeling her fingers curl around his. 'But if we do this… I can't stay with you, Arianna.'

She nodded. 'I know. And I want you to stay.'

Could she trust him to stay? He'd made it very clear that he wanted her, and maybe she didn't believe that he could sleep beside her without acting on that. Arianna stood, letting go of his hand.

'I won't be a minute.' She shot him a smile. 'I need to go and get into my pyjamas.'

'Pyjamas? Really?' The idea was oddly entrancing. But then Arianna would be just as entrancing if she chose to wear a suit of armour to bed.

'Don't worry. I'm not worried about having to fend you off in the night. I'm just giving you a minute to get undressed and get into bed, without having to fend *me* off.'

She trusted him. And even though Ben wasn't quite sure that he had the same confidence in himself, he knew that Arianna's trust would stop him from making a move. He watched her go, smiling at the thought.

He took off his clothes, slipping under the

covers. Arianna returned in an oversized pair of striped pyjamas, which somehow failed to obscure her lithe frame and the way she moved. And then they were together. Separated by layers of bedclothes, but together in ways that really mattered.

'I'm not sure that anyone could have a nightmare here.' He put his arm around her and she snuggled against him.

'I don't think so either.' She smiled up at him. 'Maybe that's the trick of it. If you dare the nightmares to come, then they don't. It's falling asleep dreading them that lets them in.'

'I don't know. Do you dare them?' Ben wondered if she would. It seemed to him to be a step forward from fearing them.

'Yes. I dare them. They can't get me here.'

He hoped not, with all his heart. Ben held her, listening to the sound of the sea, until she drifted off to sleep.

Arianna had slept soundly until dawn. Ben had carefully disentangled her from his arms, and slipped out of bed to get dressed and make coffee for her. As he brought the mugs out of the kitchen, he saw her stir.

She sat up and stretched. Ben managed to negotiate the muslin curtains without spilling the coffee and she took one of the mugs from him.

'Thank you. This is really nice.'

It was. He sat down on the bed, stretching his legs out in front of him, and Arianna caught up a pillow with her free hand, putting it behind his back. It was like the lazy intimacy that came after a night of passion, only spiced with the sharp tang of unrequited desire. But Ben had told himself that he wasn't going to think about that…

'How did you sleep?'

'Like a baby.' She took a sip of her coffee and Ben chuckled.

'You mean waking up at three-hour intervals, wanting to be fed?'

She wrinkled her nose. 'Like a five-year-old, then. You know, when Jonas just keels over and goes to sleep when he's tired.'

'Funny, I don't recall you kicking me in the night. Or waking up with your elbow in my ribs.' Ben wouldn't have minded any part of her coming into contact with any part of him. Having her close, knowing that she was safe in his arms, had helped him to sleep and he'd woken in the cool breeze of the morning feeling rested and refreshed.

'Would you like to take my car this morning? You could bring Jonas down to play on the beach, before you come to meet me at the health centre. He might like to stop off and make a few refinements to his water cascade.' She pointed towards the arrangement of beakers and water conduits that still occupied one corner of the veranda.

'Yes, I think he probably would. You're sure you don't need it?' This really ought to feel odd, and yet it was somehow perfectly natural. Drinking coffee together and discussing their day. Working out who was going to take the car…

'No. It's a lovely morning and I think I'll walk down to the health centre. I could do with the exercise.'

CHAPTER NINE

WHEN BEN ARRIVED at the health centre, Andreas and Eleni were waiting for them. Andreas presented Jonas with his very own fishing line, and the three of them left, Jonas chattering excitedly.

'He'll be all right with them.' Arianna seemed keen to reassure him.

'He's fine. He's been looking forward to this all morning.'

Ben ought to feel more guilty about this than he did. He'd always made sure that his holidays and weekends were set aside as time spent with Jonas, but he had to admit that the boy was really enjoying this holiday. He was safe, and loving the attention from both Arianna and the community in the village.

Maybe he was just a little sensitive about it because every moment with Arianna was so precious, and he had to keep reminding himself that he was taking nothing away from his son. He followed Arianna to the car, deciding that perhaps he was overthinking things.

The manager met them in the reception area of the hotel, leading them out past the pool and to a cluster of small guest houses, nestled in the shade of large trees.

'We have another two children that the parents are concerned about. I've isolated them and checked everyone now, and there are only a few of our senior guests who have not been vaccinated.'

'You asked if they had measles when they were children?' Arianna was walking beside him, an intent expression on her face, and Ben guessed she wasn't much looking forward to this next patient consultation.

'They all said they did.'

Arianna nodded. 'In that case they're most likely to be immune. Thanks for doing all that; you seem to have things well under control.'

The manager shot her a rueful smile. 'All except Mr and Mrs Colyer. Mr Colyer is still angry this morning.'

Arianna rolled her eyes. 'Well, *angry* isn't

going to solve anything. Let's see if we can come up with something that does.'

The guest houses were the height of understated luxury inside, and Ben began to feel a little less guilty about having been offered a suite here. That was nice, but these were fantastic. But when the manager introduced him to Jem Colyer, he could see straightaway that the hotel's gesture had done nothing to appease him. He shook Ben's hand, ignoring Arianna completely.

'I'm glad to see they've called you in to take a look at Eloise, Dr Marsh. I've been banging my head against a brick wall with these hotel people.'

'I've not exactly been called in, Mr Colyer. I work in London and I'm not licensed to practise here in Greece. I'm here as a matter of courtesy to Dr Petrakis and as an observer only.' He had to make that clear right from the very start.

'Then perhaps you can observe that we're not at all happy about this.' Jem frowned.

'This is lovely, much nicer than the room we had.' Eloise's mother caught her husband's arm. 'Calm down, will you, Jem.'

'There's nothing to be calm about, Kriss.' Jem glowered at his wife and she let go of his arm. 'I was looking on the internet last night and Greece had an outbreak of measles a couple of years ago. She's caught it here, and the hotel didn't warn us. Don't you think they should refund our money?'

'Dr Petrakis is here to see your daughter, Mr Colyer.' Ben decided to avoid the issue of the hotel's culpability for the time being. 'I think that's the most important thing at the moment.'

'Yes. Of course.' Jem seemed to deflate a little, letting Kriss lead Arianna and Ben out of the main living area, and to their daughter's room.

'I'm sorry about Jem. He gets worked up about things. Especially when it comes to Eloise.'

Arianna was looking at her thoughtfully. She'd not said a word since they'd arrived, and Ben reckoned she must be standing back to look at the interactions between the couple.

'That's all right. Let's take a look at Eloise and see how she's feeling today, shall we?'

She took a pair of gloves from her bag, putting them on. Then she pulled a chair up beside Eloise's bed. The little girl smiled up at Arianna when she recognised her.

'Hello, Eloise. How are you feeling today? You've still got that runny nose, I see.'

Eloise nodded miserably, rubbing her eyes, and Arianna caught her hand, stopping her. 'Your eyes hurt you?'

Another nod.

'Okay, sweetie. I know it's hard but you must try not to touch them. I'll show your mum how to bathe your eyes for you, and then they'll feel much better. And we'll keep the curtains closed, shall we, so it's not so bright in here.'

Kriss hurried to the window, and Arianna smiled up at her. 'Leave them for a couple of minutes, please, until I've examined her.'

'Yes. Yes, of course.'

Arianna carefully checked Eloise's mouth, and Ben saw the characteristic greyish-white spots on the inside of her cheeks. The little girl fretted a bit as Arianna sat her up and removed her pyjama top. The measles rash hadn't appeared yet, but everything else confirmed Arianna's diagnosis.

'Measles. Definitely.' He supposed he should say something. Arianna shot him a smile.

'But she doesn't have a rash…' Kriss frowned.

'No, sometimes the rash doesn't appear straightaway. But Eloise's other symptoms are unmistakable, and by tomorrow she may well be showing signs of a rash. You're giving her the medication I gave you yesterday? Her temperature is a little high.'

Kriss began to blush. 'I gave her the first dose, before she went to sleep last night. Jem said not to give her any this morning. The label on the bottle is in Greek and we can't read it, you see.'

Ben saw Arianna take a breath. Clearly she was holding her own irritation in check. 'This is exactly the same medication that she'd be given in England. Children's paracetamol or ibuprofen will help bring her temperature down, and make her more comfortable, so you're really not doing her any favours by withholding it.'

'Yes. Yes, of course.' Kriss turned to Ben. 'Would you tell Jem that, please?'

Another glance from Arianna. She could easily, in her position as the doctor in attendance, have insisted she tell Jem that herself. But he'd already seen that Arianna's patients came first for her, and she gave Ben a nod.

'Yes, Mrs Colyer. I'll tell him.' If that didn't work, Ben might just take Jem out and dunk him in the swimming pool.

Arianna watched as Kriss measured out a dose of the syrup and gave it to Eloise, then showed her how to bathe the little girl's eyes with damp cotton wool. There was so much care there, so much genuine warmth, that by the time she'd finished Eloise had begun to talk to her, and professed herself to be feeling much better now.

'You're looking lots better as well. I'll come and see you tomorrow, to check on you.'

It wasn't really necessary; Eloise showed no signs of any complications and measles didn't really require three doctor's visits. But Arianna obviously felt that the family wasn't dealing with this well, and Ben shared her concern.

They'd done all they could for Eloise, but there was still unfinished business. Arianna leaned towards Kriss, asking if there was somewhere private they might talk, and

Kriss nodded. She led them through a glass-paned door onto a small veranda, leaving the door open so that she could hear if Eloise needed anything. Ben followed, reluctant to leave Arianna on her own to talk with either Kriss or Jem.

'Is there something bothering your husband?' Clearly she'd seen what Ben had also noticed, and that a case of measles wasn't the most pressing of this family's problems.

'It's… It has nothing to do with this.'

'It seems to be affecting his reactions, now.'

Kriss slumped down into a seat, and Arianna perched herself on the edge of the seat next to her, so that she could be face to face with her.

'We…lost a pregnancy eighteen months ago. Jem took it very hard.'

'I'm sorry to hear that. It must have been hard for both of you.'

Kris nodded, a tear running down her cheek. 'Yes, it was. We got through it and we were going to try again, but…then last year Jem lost his grandmother. He was very cut up about it; his gran gave him a home and brought him up after his parents died. It was expected, she had cancer, but he never got a chance to say goodbye to her, because of last summer's lockdown restrictions.'

Arianna nodded. 'That must have been very difficult for him.'

She was calm and quiet, giving Kriss a chance to talk. And Kriss seemed to be responding to her.

'He's so angry. He was angry with the doctors, because they wouldn't let him see his gran. Angry with the world. He cares so much about Eloise, and he just wants to wrap her in cotton wool all the time. He tried to get us a flight home last night, but none of the airlines would take us, with her being sick like this. Being isolated again is pushing all of his buttons, and he's worried about what it'll cost to stay on here, and whether he'll be docked pay for any extra time he takes off work.'

Kriss pulled a crumpled paper handkerchief from her sleeve, and started to snuffle into it.

'All right, let's take one thing at a time. See if we can't tick a few things off the list. I think you may well have to stay on for a little while. Eloise shouldn't be in contact with anyone until at least five days after her rash has appeared, and even then I won't be able to sign her off to travel if she's still unwell. But I'll make sure that the hotel doesn't charge you for the extra time you spend here. Kriss looked up at her questioningly and Arianna smiled. 'Being the daughter of the owner here does have its perks.'

'Thank you. I'm sorry about what Jem said about that yesterday.' Kriss looked up at Ben. 'That's why you've brought Dr Marsh with you?'

'He's here to help. That's what I want to do as well. I can write a letter for your husband's employers, saying that I've diagnosed Eloise and instructed that she must stay here and isolate. Maybe you can use it to claim from your holiday insurance, if he loses any money.'

'Yes…thank you, I didn't think of that. I'll have a look at the documents.' Kriss nodded, managing a watery smile. Clearly Arianna's approach was working, and any moment now she'd get around to the most important part of the issue.

'I'm a lot more concerned about your husband's state of mind, though. Has he spoken to anyone about how he feels about the death of his grandmother?'

Right on cue. That was what Ben was most concerned about as well.

Kriss's face fell. 'He won't. He just bottles it all up and rages about everything else. And everyone had a hard time of it last year…'

'Yes, that's true, everyone did. That doesn't mean that he can't ask for help if he's experiencing difficulties. Do you think you could speak to your doctor about this? Either together, with your husband or on your own?'

Kriss shook her head. 'No. Jem doesn't like him and, to be honest with you, I don't feel I get through to him either.'

Ben cleared his throat and Arianna looked up at him, her slight nod giving him the go-ahead to add his own contribution to the conversation.

'Where do you live, Kriss?' He reckoned he heard a London accent in her speech.

'London. Docklands. Why?'

'My practice isn't too far from there. If you'd like to make an appointment with me, then we could talk over some of the things that might help your husband come to terms with what's happened.'

Kriss hesitated. 'I…don't know. I really don't think I can get him to come.'

'Then you come alone. This is obviously affecting you too.' Ben tore a leaf from his notebook, jotting down his work number and the name of his practice and giving it to Kriss.

'Okay. Yes, I will. Thanks.'

It was the most he could do. Jem Colyer obviously needed help; his anger and grief were spilling over and tainting the rest of his life. Ben could understand that; when Emma had died his own grief had been so overwhelming that sometimes anger had felt like a relief. But he'd known that it wasn't an answer. He hoped that Kriss would take him up on his offer and that he'd see her again.

'Is there anything else that we can do for you, Kriss?' Arianna's tone was gentle.

'No I'm… I'm grateful for what you've done already. I should get back to Jem, before he says something he shouldn't to the manager…' Kriss was gnawing at her lip now, obviously under stress, and she led the way back through Eloise's bedroom and into the main seating area.

Jem had obviously already said something he shouldn't. The manager was standing stiffly by the large windows, clearly looking forward to making his escape, and Jem was slumped in an armchair, seemingly alone with his thoughts. You could have cut the atmosphere with a knife.

Arianna smiled up at Ben, and the warmth in her eyes burned away all of his frustration. He took a deep breath and walked over to Jem.

'Mr Colyer. I know that you're concerned about your daughter and I'd like to set your mind at rest.' He waited for Arianna to sit down and then took the seat opposite Jem's armchair.

'Too right I'm concerned.' Jem smirked at Arianna, as if he imagined that she was about to get her comeuppance, and she smiled back at him pleasantly.

'I'm not licensed to practise medicine in Greece, but I am a doctor—'

'That's all right. I'll take *your* word for it.'

Why? Arianna was a fine doctor, and Jem

was being blatantly insulting. Ben swallowed the question down.

'Well, I've observed the examination that Dr Petrakis carried out today, and I concur with her diagnosis of measles.'

'That's pretty obvious; it doesn't need two doctors to tell me that. I'm a bit more worried about the medicine she gave Eloise.' Jem jutted his chin aggressively.

'The standard treatment for measles is paracetamol or ibuprofen, to reduce your daughter's temperature and make her feel more comfortable.' Ben decided to leave out the part about medicines being subject to international standards. 'It's exactly the same preparation as you'd be able to buy from a chemist in England.'

'The picture on the box is the same as the one in our cabinet at home. Eh, Kriss?' Jem looked up at his wife and she pursed her lips, clearly feeling a little impatient with her husband. 'It might have been different, though.'

'Yes, it might. But I can reassure you that it's not.' Ben resisted the temptation to roll his eyes. 'Dr Petrakis has advised that your daughter be kept in quarantine, as measles is exceptionally infectious, but I believe she intends to exert her influence here and make sure that you're not charged any extra for staying a little longer.'

Jem's lip curled. 'That's another thing. If she's the daughter of the bloke who owns this place she's bound to want to keep us sweet, isn't she?' He turned to Arianna. 'I can tell you now that I'll be putting in a complaint. Like I said, my daughter's picked this up here and we should get compensation.'

Keeping things friendly was one thing. Allowing Arianna to be bullied like this was quite another, and Ben wasn't going to leave her to defend herself. He cleared his throat, and Jem looked back at him.

'I'd encourage you to ask for anything you feel you're entitled to, but I gather you'd been here for ten days when Dr Petrakis saw your daughter yesterday and she was displaying symptoms then. The incubation period for measles is ten to fourteen days, so it's most likely that she contracted it at home.'

Jem thought for a moment. Ben allowed himself to wonder if he was struggling with fourteen minus ten, because it took his mind off the sudden need to protect and defend Arianna.

'Yeah, okay. I see your point, doc. I just want to stand up for my rights, you know?'

Ben nodded. 'I understand that. Are there any other concerns that we can help you with?'

'Nah, I suppose we're good.' Jem stood up, making for the French windows that led out onto the patio. 'I need a bit of fresh air. But I'll be expecting you to come back and see how my Eloise is doing.'

'Dr Petrakis will be coming to see your daughter again tomorrow. You have her number so you can call if you're worried about anything.'

Jem didn't answer, wrenching open the doors and walking outside.

'Yes. We have your number. Thanks.' Kriss grimaced apologetically. 'He's very stressed...'

'It's okay. I'll see you tomorrow. You take care, eh? And call me if you need me.' Arianna rose, giving Kriss a smile. The manager made for the door with as much speed as he could without breaking into a run, and ushered them out.

* * *

The manager wrung Ben warmly by the hand, before giving the room numbers for her other two patients to Arianna and hurrying away. Ben watched his receding figure, as he walked around the swimming pool and back into the hotel.

'Nice guy. Was he like that yesterday?' Ben stopped in the shade of one of the trees, looking out to sea.

'Worse.' Arianna shook her head. 'There's something about him, though. As if all the shouting is really a scream of pain.'

'I just wish that he hadn't felt the need to attack you. That really wasn't fair.'

'He's afraid. He wants to protect his wife and daughter, and he's just lashing out at anyone and anything.'

Arianna was right. She'd borne the brunt of the insults and her ability to look past that and try to help the family was commendable. 'I know. I felt a lot like that when Emma died.'

Arianna leaned towards him. 'I'll bet you didn't go as far as interfering with Jonas's medical treatment, though. Or making the people around you walk on eggshells.'

Ben shook his head. 'No. No, I didn't do that. Jem really needs some help, for his own sake and his family's.'

'Yes, he does. I'll do whatever I can, and maybe Kriss will help him to make the right decision and come and see you, when you get back to England. It was really good of you to offer that.'

Ben smiled down at her. Being treated with such contempt can't have been easy for her, but it was just like Arianna to push her own feelings to one side and concentrate on what other people needed. She did it a little too much for her own good sometimes; he felt sure that ignoring her own feelings was the root cause of the nightmares that plagued her.

'I'll come back tomorrow, when you go to see Eloise.'

She raised an eyebrow. Maybe that had sounded far too protective, but Ben didn't actually care. He *did* feel protective about Arianna, and it was the first time in years that he'd begun to believe he could make a difference.

'You're on holiday, remember.'

'Yeah. Just taking a little holiday from my holiday. A beautiful island bathed in sunshine can begin to grate a little after a while.'

'I wouldn't know. This beautiful island *is* where I work, so I suppose I have the best of both worlds. And I wouldn't have missed your spectacular self-control for the world.'

Ben grimaced. 'It wasn't that obvious, was it?'

'No, it wasn't obvious at all. You were firm with him, but you were really kind as well.'

An idea occurred to Ben. 'Tell you what. Lizzie's taken a liking to one of the cocktails they do here. It doesn't contain any alcohol, so you can drink as many as you like and still drive, but it has umbrellas and cherries...'

'Umbrellas and cherries. Sounds good to me.' Arianna grinned.

'What do you say we go to see how the other two kids are doing, and then go upstairs to my room and order room service. We'll drink the cocktails and you can tell me exactly how annoying this afternoon's been. As loudly as you like.'

She was thinking about it. It was nice to

see Arianna acknowledging her frustration instead of bottling it all up.

Suddenly she smiled, reaching up to caress his cheek, and Ben felt a tingle of excitement radiate from her touch. 'Letting off steam over cocktails. You know my guilty pleasures, don't you?'

He could think of a more delicious way of letting off steam. And as to guilty pleasures...

Cocktails were going to have to do.

Arianna had diagnosed one of the other children with measles, and Ben had concurred. The second had a runny nose but none of the other symptoms, and since he'd been vaccinated they'd agreed that it was unlikely he would have been infected. She'd already checked her records, to make sure that all of the children on the island had been inoculated, and it seemed that the outbreak was under control.

They ate at the hotel that evening, with Lizzie and James. Arianna had started to worry what Lizzie might be thinking of her, but her fears were groundless. Lizzie had the same laid-back sense of humour as her brother, and they were laughing together before very long.

Ben walked her out to her car. Arianna had already decided what she wanted to say to him, but he spoke first.

'You're going home alone, aren't you?'

'Yes. I… It's not that I don't want you there tonight, but I have the foundations to move forward now.'

'And that's something you have to do by yourself.' A flash of regret showed in his eyes.

'Maybe not entirely but… I don't want to define our relationship any more, Ben. You were there for me when I needed you, and I'm really grateful for that. But…' She shrugged, not entirely sure how to explain this to him.

'I get it. We both made very firm limits for ourselves, and I couldn't have stayed with you all night without them. But they feel like restrictions on our friendship now.'

That was exactly how Arianna felt. Being able to hold him at night, but not able to do so for anything other than comfort. Being able to touch him, but not in the way that she wanted. The glimmer in his eyes now was telling her that it wasn't in the way *he* wanted either.

'Let's start again, Ben. I'd rather go back to the beginning and have a friendship with you that can just go wherever it goes. One where we don't feel we're rescuing each other from anything.'

He chuckled. 'Anything apart from each other, you mean.'

They were still there. Her doubts and his, about whether they'd ever be able to be more than just friends. Neither of them were ready for that yet, but at least it was something that was possible now.

Arianna turned to get into her car but he stopped her, laying his fingers gently on her arm.

'Would it be too soon…?'

'No. It wouldn't.' Not a moment too soon. Arianna stood on her toes, planting a kiss on his lips and then drawing back again.

Just a few seconds. That somehow made it even more intense. When he brushed a kiss against her cheek it felt as if the world was slowly exploding, shockwaves almost bringing her to her knees. There was something to be said for restraint, even if it was hard.

'Goodnight. Sleep well.' His eyes were luminous in the half light.

'You too, Ben. Shall I call you when I get home?'

'Yeah, I'd like that. Just to let me know that you're okay. And if you need me...'

'I know. You're only a call away.' She wasn't going to need him tonight. Because need precluded this delicious wanting, and that was more important to her than anything.

'Quick. Go.' He smiled down at her. 'Before I decide that I'm not done rushing things.'

She got into her car, reversing out of the parking space. Trying to watch Ben and drive at the same time wasn't going to work, and so she dragged her gaze back onto the road in front of her. But when she glanced in her rear-view mirror he was still standing there, watching her go.

They'd talked on the phone for an hour before Arianna had gone to sleep. Ben had been there for her when she'd needed him, and now missing him at night had become a matter of quite a different kind of longing. Arianna was determined that if he did end up in her bed again, it wouldn't be out of pity or concern.

'What do you reckon?' She was walking through the reception area of the hotel with Ben, after they'd visited Eloise for the second time together.

'She's not well, but there's nothing to worry about. She should be ready to travel in a little over a week, and Jem and Kriss can take her home.'

'Yes. I think so too.' Arianna looked up at Ben. 'Why are we not happy about that?'

'Because Eloise isn't the one who needs real help.'

'Yes. I don't see what more we can do for Jem, though.' He had seemed calmer and quieter today, and had been positively friendly towards Arianna. But she still had the feeling that nothing had changed with him, and he might explode into another show of anger if he felt his wife and daughter were threatened again.

'Neither do I. Kriss has given me her mobile number and I'll give her a call when I get back to London and see how they're doing.'

'That's nice of you. At least I don't feel as if I'm sending them off into a void.' She sighed. Eloise was very well cared for and there really was nothing more that they could do. 'So what are you up to now?'

'Jonas has discovered the ball pit in the hotel basement. He's completely lost interest in fishing now, and he wants me to build him one when we get home. I'm going to see if I can wrangle him out of there to have some lunch. You?'

'I'm going for a bite to eat, and then picking up some trees. We're going to plant them in the courtyard at the front of the health centre, and the land at the back as well. I've raised the money for it all, and people from the village are coming to help.'

Ben gave her a quizzical look. 'Let me get this right. Your father built and equipped one of the best health centres I've seen anywhere, and you're spending time raising money for a few trees?'

'It does look like a bit of an oversight, doesn't it? But you raise the money, and then go and plant the tree yourself, and it gives you ownership of a place.'

'Ah, yes, that works. I'd suggest it at our next practice meeting if we had any room for trees. Would you like a hand?'

She was hoping he might say that. 'Everyone's welcome. You have to dig if you want lemonade.'

'No problem there; I can dig. I don't suppose you need any more trees, do you?'

Arianna had intended to buy some of the trees herself; it had taken a while to raise the money she had. 'I think we could do with a few extra. Why, would you like to donate one?'

'I think I'd like that very much. I'd better get two, though, because Jonas will want his own. As long as no one minds—this is a project for the village.'

'No one minds.' And Arianna really liked the idea that Ben would be leaving a tree behind, at the health centre. She could tend it and watch it grow, and maybe one day he'd be back, to see it blossom and bear fruit.

'That's great, thanks. Shall we go and have something to eat, then we can leave Jonas here while we pick up the trees and pop back to fetch him?'

She liked the way that planning anything with Ben was so effortless. It was as if she was a part of their small family, and she'd never been a part of a family that had so much fun together.

'Yes, let's do that. Then you can come and decide which square foot of Ilaria you'd like to make your own.'

CHAPTER TEN

ARIANNA HAD TOLD Ben that she hadn't had a nightmare in a week. She didn't jump at the sound of the ferry's horn, and she was happy to spend time on the water. She seemed rested and relaxed, and for now the memories of the day on the ferry had loosened their grip on her. It might not last, but it was progress. She knew there was a way out now and however many setbacks she encountered, she could work her way back again from them.

That brought a whole new set of challenges. The one where they'd taken Jonas swimming in the hotel's swimming pool and he'd felt the subtle brush of her limbs against his. The one where he'd watched her on the boat, the sea breeze caressing her body. He'd never actually reckoned that a breeze was something to be jealous of before. Oh, and whenever she turned her dark eyes on him and smiled. That was when his whole world tipped into a maelstrom of forbidden possibilities.

He missed their nights together, though. Waking early to find her sleeping beside him had touched Ben deeply. But it had just been a way of being close to her, and yet still keeping himself safe from the conflicting realities of a relationship. Now that their relationship had changed, he hadn't dared go any further than a brief kiss goodnight, and long phone calls before they went to sleep.

Arianna had cooked for Lizzie and James tonight. It had been a good evening, Arianna and Lizzie were becoming great friends and they'd been talking together in the kitchen for a long while, leaving him and James to drink their coffee on the veranda, and keep an eye on the children.

Lizzie had begun to yawn, and declared her interest in an early night. James had called the hotel's taxi service and they'd taken the children with them, telling Ben and Arianna that they didn't want to put an end to the evening for them. Arianna's smile had made it impossible for Ben to leave.

They sat in silence on the veranda, watching the sun go down. 'I'm just wondering if I could ever tire of this. Do you?' Ben asked.

'No, not really. A nice sunset always does it for me. When I was in London and I took the bus to work, I used to always look up from my book when we were crossing London Bridge. The view was always the same, and always different.'

Ben nodded in agreement. 'I always get that feeling when I'm walking past St Paul's. Different skies on different days, but it's always the same.'

'But you only have another week here. You should catch every sunset.'

Every smile and every word that Arianna said too. Each time she surprised him, and whenever he knew what she was about to say or do.

'What do you say…we make the most of the week we have left?' She turned towards him suddenly. This time, Ben knew exactly what she meant.

'I'm not sure that's a good idea, Arianna.' The sudden stiffness in his tone sounded like a rejection, when really all he wanted to do was to gather her up in his arms and make sweet love to her. 'I care too much about you, and…'

'And what?'

'We've only known each other for two weeks.'

Arianna shot him a reproving glance. 'We've known each other for most of our lives, Ben.'

It felt like that to him as well. 'I'm going back home in a week.'

'That's okay. Your place is in London and mine's here. We both respect that.'

Ben was beginning to lose all respect for it. Wondering if he might not fall on his knees and promise to move here, lock, stock and barrel, just to be with Arianna. But that was impossible. He wanted to make promises to Arianna, could even imagine himself doing so, but he still couldn't be sure that he could keep them.

'You know I care about you, Arianna. But—'

'I know. You don't want to hurt me.' She shook her head, smiling. 'Haven't you been listening at all? If you want to protect me, then you should make a start by respecting my decisions.'

She was right, of course. They'd already taken the step of wanting to find out where their friendship would lead, and they'd both known in their hearts that it would be here. He was fresh out of excuses, and he couldn't pretend to himself or Arianna that he didn't want her.

Her bag was hanging over the back of her seat, where she'd left it after rummaging through it to find something for Lizzie. She reached into it, taking something out and concealing it in her hand.

'This isn't a warm night, or a sunset, or a glass of wine with dinner talking, Ben. I've thought about this and it's what I want. I think it's what you want too, but you won't allow yourself to because you *are* going home in a week, and you're too much of a gentleman.' She held up a condom.

He was *not* thinking anything remotely gentlemanly at the moment. 'Have you got just one of those?'

'What do you think? I'm a doctor, and this is a very large bag. I should probably warn you that I'm fully prepared to take advantage of you.'

'Come here…' His head was swimming, with a desire so strong that it almost frightened him.

She got to her feet and walked over to him. Her gaze never leaving his face, she slowly sat down on his knee. Ben reached for her, pulling her close, and kissed her. Hard and strong, feeling her respond hungrily.

'That's what I really like about you, Ben. Underneath, you're not a gentleman at all…'

This was so much better than she'd thought it could be, which sent the feeling firmly into the realms of the unknown. Her whole body was alight with desire and when she pressed the condom into his hand, and he took it, a bright feeling that they could do anything they wanted together consumed her.

'Shall I make the bed up here?' She wanted to make love with him in the cool evening breeze.

'I don't think I can let you go for that long…' His lips curled wickedly. She felt his fingers skimming the fabric of her dress and then his hand on her breast. He kissed her and the effort it took not to scream out loud seemed to concentrate her hunger for him.

'Good thought. My bedroom, then...' Her fingers found the button at the waistband of his trousers, and she heard the soft swish of the zip. A strangled groan escaped his lips.

He threaded his fingers through her hair, letting her just enjoy his kisses, and the feeling that he was all hers and that she could do whatever she wanted with him. He responded to her every touch, his body hard and his mouth possessive. It almost broke her, right there and then.

'Arianna.' It was his turn now, and he was working slowly and steadily down the buttons at the front of her dress. He lifted her to her feet, slipping the fabric from her shoulders and running his fingers over the lace edges of her panties and bra.

His grin told her that he liked what he saw, very much. And when he reached for her, running his hands along the curve of her waist, she began to tremble.

'Ben... Now...'

He leaned forward, kissing her forehead. 'Soon.'

He was tender, but she knew he could be passionate. And right now Arianna wanted passion. She reached forward, grasping the open front of his shirt. 'Now, Ben. Don't hold back on me now.'

He pulled her close again, and she coiled her arms around his neck. When he lifted her, she wound her legs around his waist and he carried her to her bedroom, a delicious friction zinging between them as he moved.

He laid her down on the bed, and she watched him undress. Beautiful. Pale golden skin, smooth and touched by the sun. The kind of body that a woman could worship, slim hips and long limbs, knitted together by the hard ripple of muscle. And he was looking at her as if she were the most desirable woman in the world.

When he joined her on the bed she goaded him, whispering in his ear to tell him exactly what she wanted from him. Warmth bloomed in his pale eyes and he pulled back for a moment, slipping her panties off. The condom took only a moment and then he leaned in again, kissing her mouth.

Passion fired between them. One hand

curled around her leg, pulling it upwards so that he could sink deeper inside. The other slid behind her back, hooking around her shoulder so that there was no escaping the almost unbearable joy of each thrust of his hips. She saw him grit his teeth, making an effort to stay in control as the wild passion in his eyes built. And then she saw nothing, her eyes squeezed shut against the rolling, spreading pleasure as her body surrendered to his.

'Open your eyes. Please...' As the wild pulse of desire began to subside, she felt him nuzzle against her shoulder, whispering in his ear. When she looked up at him, taut muscle and tendon showed that he was near breaking point. Arianna wrapped her legs around him, feeling sharp aftershocks of pleasure pulse through her body as he reached his own climax.

They were both too breathless for words, hearts beating against each other's chest. He kissed her, taking her with him as he rolled over onto his back. She felt him reach around her, unhooking her bra, so that she could slip it off and there was nothing to stop his skin from touching hers. Arianna began to doze, knowing that tonight was very far from over.

Then she felt his hand, smoothing her curls away from her face. 'That was…beyond anything, Arianna.'

'Yes, it was.' He'd demanded a response that she hadn't even known she was capable of. And the knowledge that it had shaken him too, that he couldn't truly put the force of their passion into words either, warmed her. She kissed his cheek, and he smiled lazily.

'Do you want to sleep now?' The light in Ben's eyes told her that he already knew the answer.

'No.'

'You want to play, then?'

Ben's idea of play was scintillating. Hushed voices, talking and laughing together. Watching the strong lines of his body in the soft light from the lamp beside the bedside, as the arms of the ceiling fan revolved slowly. Letting him find out exactly what her body could do, and exploring his. And when finally he tipped her onto her back, and they were joined in the most satisfying way possible, it was just the beginning of a slow, delicious climb back into mindless passion.

'Do you always like to be on top?' she teased him as they lay curled together on the bed. Their own little world, lit by the tender glow of lamplight.

'I'd like to watch you on top of me…' He kissed her tenderly.

'Mm. I'd like that too. Or standing up. Sitting down…'

He chuckled. 'On our sides, so I can touch every part of you. Sixty-nine different things.'

'It's a lot to get through.' Arianna snuggled against him. 'You think a week will be enough?'

'We have time management skills.' He pulled her close, wrapping his arms around her. 'Now's the time for sleep, sweetheart.'

She snuggled against him, falling into a deep, dreamless sleep.

It seemed as if Ben had lived his whole life here. He was getting to know the people in the village and understood a few Greek words now. He knew the best places to shop for food, and when the fishing boats returned with their cargo. And the last four nights had been indescribable. They'd thrown themselves into making the best of what little time they had, and there had been times when Ben had actually thought it was possible to pass out from an overload of pleasure.

He walked up to the health centre to meet Arianna from work. She was sitting in the reception area alone, her face glowing.

'What?' He let go of Jonas's hand, and the boy ran over to Arianna for a hug.

'I… I called my father.'

'You did?'

There was no need to ask whether Arianna's call to her father had gone well. It was written all over her face.

'I called at lunchtime. He was in a meeting but I left a message and he called me straight back, about two minutes later.'

Just what Ben would have done if it had been his child calling him. Jonas ran over to the toy box in the corner, which was his usual port of call when they came here, and Ben sat down to listen to Arianna.

'We talked a bit. A lot, actually, we were

on the phone for nearly an hour. He told me all about his plans for the hotel on Kantos.'

'Nothing else?'

She grinned. 'You don't know my father. He always keeps his business interests very close to his chest. Going into details is quite something for him.'

'Okay. Whatever works. Did you tell him all about your work? Your latest brilliant diagnosis?'

'No. I told him about the trees we'd planted. He said he thought it was a really good way of involving everyone.'

Ben had felt it was rather more a labour of love. But Arianna seemed pleased, and that was all that mattered.

'So…you're going to talk again?' That was the main thing. That Arianna's initiative wouldn't be lost, and that she could make her peace with her father.

'Yes, he's going to call me a week on Sunday. He's put it in his diary. Not because he might forget, but to ring-fence that time. For me.'

Ben would be gone by then. But maybe he'd hear all about that conversation as well. It seemed impossible that he and Arianna could just drift away from each other.

'I'm so glad for you. I know it was a difficult step to take...' He broke off as the phone rang. That was one of the downsides of island life. There was only one doctor, and if this was someone needing Arianna's attention, their evening together would have to wait a while.

Arianna picked up the phone, speaking in Greek. As she listened, her face became troubled.

'What's the matter?' he asked as soon as she ended the call.

'Remember that guy, Jem Colyer? The family was going home today and when they were boarding the ferry there was some kind of scuffle. I don't know if anyone's been hurt, but the police are there.'

'You're going down there?' Ben didn't really need to ask.

'Yes. I don't know how long I'll be...' She flashed him a querying look. Arianna didn't need to ask either.

'Is Andreas around?'

'Yes, he can hold the fort here. He can look after Jonas too, if you want to come.'

Andreas appeared, greeting Jonas like an old friend. Ben waved to his son, telling him he'd be back soon, and then followed Arianna down to the ferry terminus.

They were both breathless when they arrived, and Arianna pushed through the people who'd been taken off the ferry, stopping at the police tape to speak to a uniformed officer then turning to Ben to relay the gist of their conversation.

'No one quite knows what caused it all. He was in the bar; apparently someone bumped into Kriss and spilled his drink on her and Eloise. Jem just snapped, and started throwing punches and then grabbed a knife from behind the bar.'

The officer spoke again in Greek and Arianna listened, nodding.

'Someone pulled Kriss away and got her and Eloise out of there, but Jem's still in the bar, threatening anyone that comes near him.'

'He's got nothing to lose now, has he?' Kriss seemed to be the stabilising factor in

Jem's life, but now that the police were keeping them apart, he might do anything.

Arianna shook her head. 'No, he hasn't. The police are hoping that Kriss may be able to talk him down a bit, but there's no way they'll let her back in there while he has a knife. There aren't too many good options left, Ben. Someone's going to get hurt.'

'We need to get in there. At least we have some idea of what's driving him.'

Arianna nodded. 'I agree. The police will escort me on, and I'll—'

'*You're* not going to do anything. I'm coming with you.'

She seemed about to argue with him, but then she flashed him a tight smile. 'I don't know why I even bothered to think you might not.'

They were given vests to wear, and a young policewoman checked that they were fitted properly then led them up the gangway and onto the ferry. It looked as if every policeman on the island had congregated on deck, but that still might not be enough to contain Jem without hurting him, particularly if he was in an uncontrollable rage.

He saw Kriss, holding Eloise. They were out of Jem's line of sight from the windows of the bar, sitting with a policewoman. The usual bustle and chatter of the ferry had given way to an almost eerie quiet. Arianna walked straight towards the officer in charge, talking to him briefly before coming back to Ben.

'I told him that we've dealt with Kriss and Jem before. He seems to think that we might have a better chance of getting through to him, he may see us as being on his side a little more than the police.'

Ben nodded. That made sense, but there was one thing he definitely wouldn't allow. 'I'll try to talk to him. I want you to stay back.'

Arianna flushed a little. 'I don't need to tell you that this is *my* practice, do I?'

'No, you don't. And I don't need to tell you that if Jem loses it completely I've got a better chance of fending him off than you do.'

She shook her head. 'I don't like it.'

'No, I know you don't. But if you could think of a reason why it shouldn't be me, you would have told me by now.' He didn't give Arianna the chance to reply, because there was always the possibility that she might get creative and come up with something. 'We should speak with Kriss first.'

She nodded, and Ben walked over to where Kriss was sitting. She was holding it together, no bewildered tears, just a grim look on her face.

'Talk to me, Kriss.' He sat down beside her.

'There's nothing you don't know already. Jem doesn't mean it. I told them that if they backed off and left him alone...'

'They can't, Kriss. He has a knife. The officer told us that it all started when someone spilled a drink.'

'Yes. It was nothing really, but Jem just blew up. I legged it with Eloise, just to get her out of the way of the scrum.'

'Is there anything else we should know, Kriss? Drink or drugs...?'

Kriss shook her head emphatically. 'No.'

'You're sure?' Arianna broke in, a worried look on her face. 'Anything he takes on prescription?'

'No, he hasn't been to the doctor in ages. He says that doctors didn't do his gran much good, which isn't entirely fair. But he likes you, Dr Marsh.'

'Really?' Ben was pretty sure he hadn't done anything to deserve that.

'He respects people who are up-front with him.'

This was only telling Ben what he already knew, that the situation was complex and that there was no one clear answer. He made no apologies for Jem, but right now his aim was to get him out of this situation in one piece. The rights and wrongs of the situation were for someone else to judge.

He questioned Kriss a little more, but she couldn't tell them anything beyond what Ben and Arianna already knew. Jem was volatile, and unpredictable. Ben walked back to the knot of police officers with Arianna.

'This isn't going to be easy.'

'And I was just thinking it would be a walk in the park.' Arianna turned the corners of her mouth down.

There was more preparation; his vest was checked again, and Arianna relayed instructions from the officer in charge of the scene. Jem was pacing up and down inside the bar, obviously becoming more agitated, and Ben had to go now if he was going to have any chance of calming Jem down.

His hand found Arianna's and he gave it a squeeze. Her whispered, *'Be safe,'* carried him through the line of policemen, and away from her. Knowing that she was watching him allowed Ben to believe that, however hopeless the situation seemed, he could succeed.

He walked to the door of the bar. Jem had stopped pacing and had returned to the bar, reaching behind it to grab a bottle and pour himself a drink. Not a good sign. He had blood on the side of his face, obviously from the fracas over the spilt drink, and he was holding a long chef's knife.

Ben knocked cautiously on the door, keeping his hands in clear sight through the glazing. Jem twitched the knife in his direction, motioning for him to come in, and Ben cautiously opened the door, stepping inside.

CHAPTER ELEVEN

WHOEVER WOULD HAVE thought that your heart could be in your mouth? Or sinking to your boots. Or inhabiting any other part of your body that it wasn't supposed to. Arianna's heart was in the same place that it had been when she was six years old and watched Ben being carried away from her on the tide. With him.

He seemed to be doing everything right, and when she looked up at the officer in charge he was nodding imperceptibly, his eyes fixed on the scene unfolding inside the bar area. Ben appeared relaxed, although the slight twitch of his fingertips showed stress. He was keeping his distance from Jem and moving slowly. Never turning his back, and concentrating all of his attention on him.

He seemed to be encouraging Jem to talk as well. At first, Ben was doing all the talking, with just nods or gestures with the knife coming from Jem. But after a while Jem started to reply to him, although Arianna had no idea what he might be saying. Ben worked his way around to the bar, perching on one of the high stools. Out of Jem's reach, and with his feet still planted firmly on the floor and ready to move, but close enough to feign some sort of connection. Arianna felt sweat trickle down her spine.

'This is taking too long.' The officer looked at his watch. It had been twenty minutes since Ben had gone into the bar, and Arianna's legs were aching with tension.

'He's still talking…' Arianna wasn't sure whether that was a good thing or not. Jem had already drained the glass at his elbow and had picked up the bottle on the bar to refill it, although Ben had clearly dissuaded him from doing so and he'd put the bottle back down again. Still talking meant that Ben was still in harm's way. Still a target.

Ten minutes more. A small patch of sweat had appeared on the back of Ben's shirt, between his shoulder blades. She loved the scent of him. Fresh sweat, hers and his, mingling with the cool smells of the night. She shouldn't think about that right now, but wasn't it always the possibility of loss that made memories so much more agonisingly clear?

A burst of static made her jump and the officer standing next to her grabbed his radio, quietening the noise and speaking in a whisper to whoever was at the other end. The hostage negotiators would be here soon, and they'd pull Ben out of there. Good for Ben, not so good for Jem, because if Ben couldn't talk him down then Arianna wasn't sure that anyone else could. Right now, she'd take good for Ben. She'd known he would go in there, but she didn't have to like it.

She heard Kriss start to sob. She'd been holding it together up till now, probably for Eloise's sake, but now the policewoman sitting next to them was trying to calm both mother and child. The officer in charge moved swiftly over, bending down in front of them and listening for a moment before guiding Kriss gently to her feet and directing two officers to go with her.

'It's best for her to go,' he responded to Arianna's questioning look. 'The child shouldn't see her father in this situation.'

A situation that could escalate at any moment. With Ben right in the thick of it. Arianna swallowed down her panic. It seemed that the police now thought that this wasn't going to end peacefully, despite all of Ben's efforts, and it was best if Kriss and Eloise didn't see what was going to happen next.

But the move wasn't without consequences. The gangway onto the ferry was visible from the bar, and Jem had looked up just at the moment that his wife ducked around the officers shielding her, trying to look back. His hand tightened around the handle of the knife and he seemed to be shouting, beating his forehead with the heel of his other hand. Ben moved, getting slowly to his feet, tension showing in his back and thighs. He was still talking, still trying to calm Jem, even though Jem was having none of it, his body coiled with aggression and his face twisted in anger. Arianna willed Ben to just get out of there. Forget about Jem and look out for himself.

Too late. Too late… Batons appeared as the police in attendance stood at the ready and

Arianna heard the click of a weapon. Jem must have seen the sudden movement and he jumped to his feet, rushing towards the door.

If he tried to fight his way through, to get to Kriss, the police would deal with Jem. Ben clearly wasn't going to let things get that far, and headed him off. Jem knocked him away but Ben seized him again, and the two men wrestled with each other before a punch to the stomach, followed through by another to the jaw, felled Jem. The knife spun away across the floor, and Ben staggered back to retrieve it.

The police surged forward and Arianna followed, desperate to make sure that Ben was all right. But as she reached the open door of the bar she saw that three policemen had Jem on the floor and Ben was kneeling next to him, still talking and obviously trying to calm Jem and inspect him for any injury. She should stay back, and let him finish what he'd started. Hanging onto his neck and kissing him could, and almost certainly would, come later.

The muffled beat of a helicopter was louder now and it was coming in close, hovering just feet above the jetty so that the men inside could jump down from it. The incident team had medics with them, who ran ahead towards the ferry.

They were taking no chances and Jem was put onto a stretcher and examined before they carried him out of the bar. Ben sat back on his heels, obviously drained by the last hour, his hand moving to his side. It was then that Arianna saw the blood.

'Ben…' She ducked past a couple of the island police, skidding to a halt next to him. He looked up at her, summoning a tight smile.

'It's okay. What is it you're supposed to say? Just a scratch.'

'You can let me be the judge of that, Ben.' Arianna loosened the vest, lifting it over his head, and saw a patch of blood on his shirt. The knife must have been deflected by the vest and sliced just below its protective shield.

'Uh… Can't you do that later?' He winced as she unbuttoned his shirt, trying to make a joke of it.

'Be quiet.' Arianna turned to call for a medical kit, but one of the officers had already thought to fetch one, and it was lying on the floor behind her. She examined the wound on his side carefully.

'How's it looking, Doctor?' His tone was still flippant, but Arianna could see pain in his eyes.

'It's superficial.' The wound was bleeding a fair bit, but it wasn't deep. Once the flow of blood was staunched, and Arianna had stitched it, he would be all right.

'I'll dress it, so that we can get you back to the health centre.' She took a wad of gauze from the medical kit, positioning it over the cut. 'Hold that there, will you, while I tape it. Keep the pressure on it.'

He did as he was told, providing the essential third hand that made any dressing easier to apply. The officer in charge of the scene cleared a path as Ben was led to a police car, and got behind the wheel himself, driving them the short way back to the health centre. He shook Ben's hand and Arianna sent him away, assuring him that there was nothing more that they needed.

The health centre was silent, and Arianna locked the main door behind them.

'Where's Jonas?'

Arianna picked up the note on the reception desk. 'Andreas and Eleni have taken him to their house. He's okay; they'll keep him occupied there. I'll get you fixed up and then you can see him, yes?'

'Yeah. Good, thanks.' He went to wrap his arms around her shoulders, and then drew back again. 'I'm sorry. There's a smudge of blood on your dress.'

'That's okay. I keep a change of clothes here and it's not the first time I've had to wash blood out of something.' She hugged him, careful not to touch the dressings on his side. Ben's chest rose and slowly fell, as if now he could finally breathe.

'I've got you, Ben,' she whispered against his chest.

'Yeah, I know. That feels so good, right now.'

She led him through to her surgery and he climbed onto the examination table, rolling stiffly onto one side. Arianna cleaned the wound, anesthetising the area in readiness for the stiches. They had to be perfect. Nothing less would do on his perfect body. She'd leave no scar, even though she wouldn't be there to see the wound knit and the mark fade. Ben lay silently as she worked.

'Done. Would you like to see before I dress it?' Arianna didn't usually offer patients that option, but it would save on a dressing because Ben would be peeling it off as soon as her back was turned.

'Yes, thanks.' He peered into the mirror that she positioned above his side, tilting it a little so that he could see. 'I'm impressed. Very neat.'

He was trying to smile but the lustre had gone from his eyes. Maybe if she waited he'd get around to saying what was on his mind. Arianna picked up his bloodied shirt, holding it up and then throwing it into the bin.

'You can't let Jonas see you in that. Andreas has a couple of scrub tops that he keeps here; he won't mind if you take one.' The V-necked blue cotton top looked enough like the casual shirts that tourists wore that once it was out of the context of the health centre it would hardly draw a second glance.

'Yes, I need to see him.' Ben started to sit up, and Arianna helped him swing his legs down from the couch.

'Of course. Not with blood on your hands, though.' Arianna took a wipe from the box on her desk, picking up his hand and carefully wiping it. However much she cleaned him up, she couldn't restore the light in his eyes, and Jonas would see that. *She* saw it, and it made her heart ache.

'Jem saw Kriss go? Is that why he got so agitated?'

'Yes. He was very on edge when I went in there, but he seemed to be getting calmer. I'd managed to persuade him that there was a way out of the situation for him, and that he didn't need to hurt himself or anyone else. Then he saw Kriss leave with Eloise, and he just flipped. He was shouting about killing anyone who got in his way.'

'So you got in his way.' Arianna tried not to show her disapproval.

'There wasn't much choice. He wouldn't have stopped, and if he'd have got out of the bar there would have been casualties.'

'There was one.'

'It was only superficial, though. You said so yourself.'

She threw the wipe into the bin, collecting

a new one to clean his other hand. 'What's going on with you?'

'I just need to see Jonas.'

Of course he did. He hadn't once said that he needed to see her, though, even though Arianna was struggling not to think that way. Of course she came second to his child; she'd never respect a man who thought differently. Being somewhere on the list would be nice, though.

'He needs to see you too. But not with blood all over you and not with that look in your eyes either. What's the matter, Ben?'

He shook his head, as if maybe that might knock his thoughts into some order. 'I've been thinking about what would have happened if I'd been more badly hurt. If I couldn't get back to Jonas...'

Arianna puffed out a breath. Not being there for the people he loved was a dilemma for Ben and probably always would be. 'You are who you are, Ben. Who you are is important for Jonas too.'

It was important to Ben. The man who believed he could no longer make a difference, and who'd made the biggest difference of all to Jem. Without Ben's intervention, the situation would have gone bad very quickly.

'Yeah.' He straightened his back, as if trying to settle a weight on his shoulders. 'It was easier when I jumped into the water after you. A lot less complicated.'

'Maybe you just thought it was. A lot of things seem less complicated when you're twelve.'

'True. Another fifteen years and perhaps I won't be worrying about Jonas so much.'

'I wouldn't count on it. I've heard reports to the contrary.' Arianna had finished cleaning his other hand, and she threw the wipe into the bin.

'Do you know what's going to happen to Jem?'

'Yes, I heard the police say that they'll be taking him to Athens initially, for a psychiatric evaluation. He'll be in a secure facility, but he'll be well looked after; I know the place. He will be charged, I don't see any alternative, but he'll have a fair hearing.'

Ben shook his head. 'I wouldn't like to be the one to make a decision about that. What

Jem did was entirely wrong, but I can still see how it all happened.'

'So can I. But we're doctors and our job isn't to make judgements; it's to do our best for people, regardless of who they are or what they've done.' She smiled at Ben. 'So I think we're off the hook with that, at least.'

He smiled, coiling his fingers around hers. 'What would I do without you to dispense stitches and good advice?'

He should go and see Jonas now. Maybe the gentle walk to Andreas and Eleni's house would finish the job of restoring his spirits. But Ben didn't seem inclined to move just yet and suddenly he reached out, wrapping his arms around her.

'Careful...'

'It's okay. I just need to hold you.' He hugged her tight, and Arianna rested her head against his shoulder.

'When Jem tried to get out of the bar, all I could think was that you were out there. I had to stop him from getting anywhere near you, Arianna.'

Maybe that was what any woman would want to hear. That a man's only thought was for her, and that he'd risk serious injury to save her. The way he'd jumped into the water after her had fuelled her fascination with Ben all these years.

But things weren't that simple now. He had Jonas to think about, and it was impossible that Ben didn't see the conflict. The things she loved most about him, his honourable nature and his bravery, might just be the things that tore them apart.

Now, in his arms, those thoughts were easy to ignore. She looked up at him, and all the warmth that had been missing from his eyes was there once more. When she kissed him, all of the yearning she felt was in his response.

'You know you'll always be my hero, don't you?'

Ben ached a little, but that was largely across his shoulders, from the tension of trying to talk Jem down. Even after the anaesthetic wore off his side didn't hurt too much, and if he took it easy for a couple of days he'd be as good as new.

He decided to tell Jonas what had happened, carefully leaving out all of the what-ifs and might-have-beens. Arianna had told Jonas that his dad had been very brave, and that the injury was just a scratch. She'd put a very large dressing on it, just to make it look a little more serious than it was.

'Phwoar, Dad!' Jonas had fallen for Arianna's version of the events hook, line and sinker, and was obviously impressed. 'Will you get a medal?'

'No. You only get a medal if you're very, very brave.'

Jonas pulled an indignant face. 'But aren't *you* very, very brave, Dad?'

'No.' The word lost its impact on Jonas, because Arianna chorused a 'Yes' at the same time.

When she heard that Ben's injury didn't preclude him from sitting up or eating, Eleni insisted that they stay for dinner. They ate under a large olive tree in the garden, with Ben propped up on cushions, and Andreas filling his plate from the serving dishes on the table. Arianna took a call, and left for half an hour to visit a feverish child, returning to say that she'd reassured the first-time mother that her little one was fine. Andreas promised to pop in and see her before work tomorrow and the business was concluded with far less fuss and more good humour than the interruption of a dinner with friends at home would have entailed. Along with all its professionalism, the health centre still retained all that was best in the community that surrounded it.

They left early, making their way slowly to Arianna's car. All Ben wanted to do was to sleep, feeling the curve of her body against his, but he should be there for Jonas tonight, to make sure that he answered any questions that the boy had.

'Dad…' It sounded as if the first of Jonas's questions was on the way. 'Can we go to Arianna's house?'

'Why do you want to go there?' Ben took his son's hand, feeling the stitches pull a little.

'So that Arianna can help me look after you.'

'Tonight, you mean?' He could see Arianna smiling out of the corner of his eye.

'Yes. Arianna, you can make sure my dad's all right, can't you?'

'Of course I can. If that's what you want me to do, Jonas.'

'Yes.'

Ben wasn't going to talk about it any more, and he certainly wasn't going to look at Arianna because he'd just start laughing. Or kissing her, and then Jonas might catch onto the fact that her motives for inviting them to stay weren't entirely medical. He reached for the car door and eased himself into his seat.

Arianna had supposed she should sleep in her own bed, leaving Ben and Jonas in the large bed in the spare room. But when it was time to put Jonas to bed, he'd asked her for a story. Ben was tired too, and he'd lain on the bed, listening as Arianna told one of the stories she remembered her father telling her and Xander.

Halfway through, a thought occurred to Jonas. 'What happens if my dad bursts his stitches? Will he bleed all over the carpet?'

'I'm not going to burst my stitches, Jonas.' Ben opened one eye.

'Oh.' Jonas looked slightly disappointed. 'Are you sure?'

'Yes, I'm sure. Arianna's stitches are very special. I'm not going to do any more bleeding, and particularly not all over the carpet.'

'Okay.' Jonas seemed happy with the explanation. He wriggled towards the side of the bed, leaving a space between himself and his father. 'You can lie here, Arianna.'

'Hey! Arianna's got her own bed, you know.' Ben's hand went to his side as he tried not to laugh.

But Jonas shot her a pleading look, and she couldn't resist. Arianna climbed onto the bed, snuggling between Ben and Jonas, and by the time she'd finished the story he was asleep.

She should go, now. But when she moved she felt Ben's hand close around hers. 'Don't. Please.'

He'd been so concerned about Jonas, but he needed a little comfort too. Carefully she snuggled against him, holding his hand between hers.

Maybe she'd wait until Ben was asleep too, and then leave. But Arianna didn't think so. It felt that this was where she was meant to be, where she would have been if fate hadn't intervened and changed the trajectory of her life. Part of a family that was stronger together than it was apart.

It couldn't happen. But, for this one night, she could pretend it might.

CHAPTER TWELVE

SOME WOUNDS DIDN'T HEAL.

The one on Ben's side was going to be fine. He was a little stiff and sore, but the sudden, unreasoning panic when he'd seen the blood had been an overreaction.

Maybe the result of a greater wound, which had been inflicted when Emma died. Mostly Ben could live with the ache, but at times like these it seemed to be draining the life blood from him. He'd tried to help Jem, because protecting his patients had become second nature to him. But he couldn't even protect the people he loved. Certainly not Emma, and now he'd taken the risk that Jonas might lose the only parent he had left, because instinct had told him that he must prevent Jem from getting anywhere near Arianna.

It was a conundrum. One that could only be solved by letting Arianna go, but that seemed impossible right now. One more wound that might never heal.

The next day was Saturday, and Arianna spent it with him at the hotel, looking after all four of the children while Lizzie and James went out sightseeing together. When there were no demands from the kids to animate her, she too seemed thoughtful and quiet.

'You're staying here tonight?' Arianna asked after they'd put the children to bed and Lizzie and James had returned to watch them.

'I could…' Perhaps she wanted to spend the night alone, to think about whatever was bugging her. Tonight suddenly seemed an impossibly long time and he drew her close, hugging her.

'Or you could come back to my place?' She turned her gaze up to meet his, and Ben could feel the echoes of the nights they'd spent together shivering through him, driving away all of the doubts and what-ifs.

'I'd really like that…'

As soon as her front door closed behind them, she kissed him. As if she was intent on driving away the silences of the day, submerging them in the chemistry that never failed them when they were alone.

'Come and lie down…' She'd been tending to him all day, making sure he didn't overdo things, but this was clearly quite a different request.

She led him into the bedroom, unbuttoning his shirt and pulling it from his shoulders. Ben let her do it, allowing these moments to blot out the past and the future, everything other than Arianna. She undressed him slowly, carefully, piling pillows so that he could recline on the bed.

'I can be *very* gentle with you.' Her fingers grazed the top button of her dress, the gesture unbearably erotic. Ben grinned.

'I'd prefer it if you left out the *very*. Maybe we could just take a little break to mop up if I start to bleed all over the carpet, eh?'

She smiled, slowly unbuttoning her dress. Stopping for one agonising minute before she let it fall to the floor at her feet.

'You've been wearing that underwear all day, and you never told me?' Ben shot her a reproachful look. Arianna's underwear was a constant fascination to him. Practical but pretty, and *very* sexy.

'I didn't want to give you ideas you couldn't follow through on...' Her wicked smile was the only thing that mattered to Ben right now.

'I can follow through. Don't you worry about that.'

She nodded, her gaze sweeping his body. It must be pretty obvious to her that he had every intention of following through, and then some. Climbing onto the bed, she kissed him lightly on the lips.

'You'll hardly feel a thing...'

He pulled her down, kissing her. Letting her feel how much he wanted her right now.

'Too late, honey. I'm already feeling something...'

Last night had been amazing. As if they'd both been trying to push back the future that they both knew was coming. Ben had driven every other thought from her head, and she knew that he was one hundred per cent there and with her.

But time was trickling through her fingers. England wasn't so very far away—Arianna's father had been known to fly to London for a meeting or a party and be back home within the space of twenty-four hours. That wasn't the issue. The problem was whether she and Ben could reach a place where they felt able to carry on their relationship, and there was so little time before he was due to leave.

She'd thought that maybe one more night, a few hours when passion drove every other thought from their heads, might allow them to gain a little perspective. But she'd woken that morning to find herself alone.

Arianna got out of bed, putting on her light cotton dressing gown. Ben was outside on the veranda, sitting staring out to sea.

'How are you doing?' She nodded towards the dressing on his side, which was visible above the waistband of his jeans.

'Fine. No problem…'

Right. That was the least of her worries settled. Arianna sat down next to him. He didn't move to pull her close, the way he usually did, and suddenly she felt very alone.

'Can we do this, Ben?'

'We *are* doing it, aren't we?'

His words smacked of denial. An attempt

to avoid the one thing that neither of them seemed to want to talk about. Only they *had* to talk about it.

'That's not what I mean. You know it.'

He nodded. 'I think the least we can do is part as friends.'

No. That would never work. Arianna took a breath, trying to steady herself. 'Knowing you, Ben…it can't ever be friendship. It's always going to be a matter of wanting you. Loving you, and being loved by you.'

She could see the pain, blooming in his eyes. 'That's something we *can't* do, Arianna.'

Then he must tell her why. Frame the reason into words for her, to give her something to hold onto.

'Why not?'

Ben turned the corners of his mouth down, staring out to sea. 'Emma…'

'You still love her?' If he did, then he should say it.

'That's not it, Arianna. I failed Emma and… I promised myself I'd do everything I could not to fail Jonas. That I'd be there for him, and protect him. The other day—it just reminded me that I can't protect both of you. And Jonas is my child; he needs me…'

Yes. She knew that. Arianna swallowed down the impulse to tell him that she needed him too. 'Do you think I could care for you if you weren't such a good father to Jonas?'

He shook his head resignedly. 'I don't suppose so.'

It was make or break now. All that Arianna could feel was grief, because it seemed impossible that this wouldn't break them apart.

'Has it occurred to you that I don't want you to protect me? I don't need you to look after me; I just want you to love me. Give me a reason why I was the one that was saved and not Xander.' The words came out in a rush of feeling and rather more honestly than Arianna had expected.

He looked at her blankly. Then suddenly his lip curled in an expression of incredulous frustration. 'Surely you don't need me to give you a reason, Arianna. If you're so blind that you can't see how important you are as a person…' He shook his head.

Then she was blind. Before she'd met Ben, her work had been the only thing she could offer to justify her place in the world. She'd begun to see a little of her own worth by looking through his eyes. But now he was going to destroy all of that, by leaving her.

'All I can see, Ben, is that you're ripping us apart.'

He knew what he was doing. Ben had held out one fragile hope that talking about things would stop the inevitable. That was gone now.

'You want to be part of that great experiment, do you? Staying together in the hope that we won't tear each other to shreds?'

She pressed her lips together. Arianna knew just as well as he did that this was exactly what would happen. He was even more determined that he had to leave, now that she'd betrayed how little she thought of herself, because Arianna needed space to grow and thrive, unhampered by his constant need to protect her.

'And you know exactly what's going to happen, do you?' She jutted her chin at him.

'No. I just know that you deserve a lot better than anything I can give you.'

She looked at him, reproachful tears in her

eyes. Then suddenly, as if she'd made a decision, she stood up.

'The trouble with you is that you saved me once, and now you think it's your job. And in case you were wondering, yes, I *do* find it infuriating.' She stamped her foot, grimacing as her bare toes hit the wooden boards. 'But you're not going to make me watch you go. I'm going out.'

He knew what she was asking, and it came almost as a relief. 'I'll be gone by the time you get back.'

'I'll leave my car keys...' One last morsel of concern that tugged painfully at his heart. He couldn't accept it; it would weaken his resolve.

'Don't. I'd rather walk back to the hotel.'

She couldn't even look at him now. Arianna turned, storming into the house, and he heard the shower running. Then silence, followed by the sound of the front door slamming shut. It was one of the many things he loved about her, that she never did anything by halves.

Ben stood for a moment, leaning on the rails that bordered the veranda. Willing himself to keep breathing and his heart to keep on beating. If he could get through these moments, stop himself from going after her and promising her anything if she would just stay with him, the next ones would be easier.

Why did doing the right thing hurt so very much?

CHAPTER THIRTEEN

WHEN ARIANNA RETURNED HOME, the house was silent. No mess in the kitchen, no sandy footprints on the veranda. It was as if Ben had never been there. She'd locked herself in her office at the health centre, throwing herself into work, and now, looking around at her empty house, she could feel the tears welling up.

She opened the fridge and surveyed its contents. Wine or ice cream? Neither of them were going to make her feel any better, and she decided on wine now, so that she could keep the ice cream for later.

She knew that Ben was right, and that it was useless. Trying to make this work would only tear them both apart. Their story had started on the day he'd rescued her, and now the fallout from that day had ended it. Arianna poured herself a glass of wine, and even after a large gulp of it she wasn't able to smile at the irony of that, because it was all too cruel.

She topped up her glass and walked out onto the veranda. Every last sign of him was gone, apart from…

Her gaze lit on Jonas's water cascade. Of course, he couldn't take that with him; it was far too complex a contraption, and would have fallen to bits if Ben had tried to move it. They'd had such fun building it.

Tears started to roll down her face and Arianna picked up her glass, heading out onto the beach. Her life, Ben's life, they'd both better be perfect from now on. Well lived, full of professional success and personal happiness. Because that was about the only thing that would ever compensate her for losing him.

Ben hurried back to his London surgery. Amalie Cutler had an appointment with him this afternoon, and he'd gone down to the hospital himself to get the test results she'd been waiting for. Her consultant was on holiday, and they'd been sitting in his in-tray for the last week. Ben had begged his secretary to give them to him, and she'd relented with a smile. When he'd opened the envelope he'd seen that it was good news.

It was the first time he'd really smiled in weeks. He'd turned the edges of his mouth up for Jonas, even laughed with his son and hugged him, the way he always did. But the staff at the busy London surgery had received short shrift, and more than one apology. He was a little busy, or a little stressed, all code-words for heartbreak. He missed Arianna with every fibre of his being, and as each day passed he only missed her more because it was longer since he'd seen her last.

But finally. This was something to smile about. Ben walked to his surgery, throwing himself into his chair and switching on his computer. Good, Amalie was first in line, so she wouldn't have to wait.

He pressed the intercom and called her name. Amalie was looking well, her blonde hair growing again after the chemo, and she'd obviously been to the hairdresser and had it cut and styled.

'How are you feeling, Amalie?'

'Good. Fine really; it's just… I'm waiting for my results. My consultant's on holiday now and, as you haven't got them back yet, I suppose they'll be another two weeks.' Amalie pursed her lips and Ben noticed the dark rings under her eyes. Waiting had obviously taken its toll.

'I've been up to the hospital and collected them. They were ready; they just hadn't been sent yet. I'm happy to tell you that it's good news.'

Amalie stared at him, her hand flying to her mouth. 'Good news? You're sure, Dr Marsh?'

'Yes, I'm sure. The tests you had at the hospital showed that your cancer is in full remission. We'll still need to see you from time to time, and I'd advise you to continue seeing your cancer nurse for support and to discuss any ongoing issues. But this is an important milestone.'

Ben handed Amalie the envelope he had ready on his desk, and she opened it with shaking hands. She stared at the sheet of paper inside blankly and then looked up at him, tears in her eyes.

'I… I don't really understand what it says.'

'That's fine. Would you like to sit quietly for a moment? Just let it sink in.' Ben suspected that anything he said now would be forgotten in the rush of emotion.

'Yes. Yes, please. I've got to call my husband and tell him. And my mum…'

'I'll get someone to make you a cup of tea, and we'll find you somewhere private for you to make your calls. Then you can come back here, and we'll discuss exactly what the letter says and what your next steps are going to be. Along with whatever it was you came to see me about today.'

'Today…?' Amalie looked at him blankly, and then smiled. 'I've not been sleeping. I've been so worried about my results and I thought I'd have a while to wait still, so I wondered if there was something you could give me, just for a couple of weeks. I don't think I'll need anything now.'

'Okay. We'll leave that then, shall we? Let me know if the sleeplessness continues…'

Amalie had already taken her phone from her bag and was obviously eager to make her calls. She got to her feet, clutching the letter to her chest as if it were the most precious thing in the world. Ben ushered her to the door but she stopped, grabbing his hand to shake it.

'Thank you so much, Dr Marsh. Not just for this but… You've been there for me all the way. You've made such a difference…'

'It's my pleasure.' Ben could hardly get the words out. The warm thrill he was feeling right now was familiar, but he hadn't experienced it since Emma had died. It had taken a trip to Ilaria to find the one person who could show him the way back to finding this feeling of fulfilment. Arianna.

Jonas had taken to the idea of board games, and every evening after tea Ben sat down with him and played draughts. Tonight, the newly established ritual didn't feel quite so painful.

'Are you cheating again, Jonas?'

'No, Dad.' Jonas looked up at him with innocent eyes.

'You're sure about that? How did your counter get from there, to there?'

Jonas studied the board carefully, and then moved his counter back to the proper place.

Ben usually allowed Jonas to win, but he tried to stay within the rules while doing so.

'What do you reckon, mate?' Ben took a sip from his glass, and Jonas picked up his juice and did the same.

'What about, Dad?'

That was always the way they started up any conversation that might lead to a decision of importance. And this decision might just be the most important of Ben's life.

'You know what taking a risk means?' Ben took two of the tiny apple cakes that his mother had brought for Jonas yesterday from the plate that lay between them on the table, putting them carefully on the table next to the draughts board. They were just beyond Jonas's reach.

'You can grab one of those easily, right out from under my nose. If you try for two, I might be able to stop you.'

Jonas thought for a moment, weighing the matter up. Then he lunged forward suddenly, grabbing an apple cake in each hand and whipping them out of Ben's reach.

'Gotcha, Dad!'

Ben smiled. There was nothing wrong with

Jonas's motor skills and he was constantly having to up his game if he wanted to out-wit the boy. Soon enough he'd be applying his full concentration to their board games and Jonas would still beat him.

'So you did. I'll have to be a bit quicker next time, won't I.'

'Yes, you *will*.' Jonas popped one of the cakes into his mouth.

It was an imperfect decision, but the same one that Ben had made when he'd plunged into the water after Arianna. Jonas was willing to take a risk, and set his eye on the greater prize. His actions weren't tempered by the fear of loss, he was a little too young to know what that really meant, but maybe that wasn't an entirely bad thing. Maybe it was the only way out of the dragging un-happiness that had followed Ben back from Ilaria, and wouldn't let him go.

'Your move, Dad.'

'Oh. Yeah, sorry.' Ben studied the board, his mind still buzzing. Was it really that sim-ple? Later on tonight, when Jonas was in bed, he'd make his decision.

* * *

Life on Ilaria wasn't all sunshine and sunsets. The sea around them held harsh realities beneath its sparkling surface. There would always be sickness and strife, disappointment and hardship. Arianna loved the slower pace of life and the beauty of her island home, along with the community who had taken her in and made her *their* doctor, not just the daughter of a man who had the money to make a difference to the island. The sunshine and sunsets weren't bad either.

But now she hardly noticed them. Her body ached when she got up in the morning, even though she'd had a full night's sleep. And the emptiness when she found that Ben wasn't there was worse than any dream.

She'd kept going, though, working hard to dull the pain. And somehow a little of Ben stayed with her. Convincing her that her life had not been saved in exchange for Xander's. His death was and always would be a tragedy, but her place in the world was hers by right.

But she *was* tired. It was late and it had been a busy week, and all she wanted to do now was to eat something and get an early night. Tomorrow was Saturday, and she had the whole weekend in front of her.

She felt her phone buzz in her pocket as she let herself into her house. Dropping her bag on the floor, she sent up a quick prayer that this *wasn't* someone who needed a doctor tonight. She pulled out her phone, looking at the screen. Ben.

Right now, a text summoning her to visit a patient would have been more than welcome, as something to take her mind off the sudden, painful hope. The fear, because she knew that Ben wouldn't get in contact with her unless it was something really urgent. The way that prickles travelled up her spine, just at the sight of his name on the small screen.

She should just delete the text without reading it. Impossible. Perhaps she'd read it and then delete it. Her fingers were trembling so much that the phone slipped through them and clattered onto the floor. Arianna retrieved it quickly, relieved to find that, although the screen had cracked, it was still working.

I want you to know that I love you. Without you I'll always be drowning.

What? Arianna looked for another text that might elaborate on that, maybe give her a clue about what to do next. She knew there wouldn't be one. Ben wouldn't ask her to do anything with this information; he'd just let her know where he stood and wait for her answer.

I love you. He hadn't said that before and neither had Arianna, although it had been on the tip of her tongue. But there had been love in everything they'd done together. Love and trust.

I'll always be drowning. That was Ben all over. The man who saved others, but who brushed the importance of that away without a second thought. He saw only the ways in which she'd saved him.

She could do this. Doing this would be the best thing she'd ever done in her life. The most difficult, terrifying, wonderful thing she'd ever done.

'Wait.' Arianna took a deep breath, admonishing herself out loud. 'Sleep on it. Call him in the morning.'

She got as far as going out to the kitchen and taking a bottle of water from the fridge, before the utter impossibility of the plan hit her. She didn't *need* to think about this. She'd known her answer from the day she'd met Ben.

Taking her phone back out of her pocket, she checked again to make sure that there wasn't another text that she'd missed. Then she dialled.

'Father…'

'Arianna?'

'I need your help…'

She heard her father catch his breath at the other end of the line. It was unusual for him to be lost for an immediate answer to anything, and when he did speak there was an uncharacteristic tremor in his voice.

'Thank you for calling me, Arianna.'

The helicopter swung low over the sea, and landed on a piece of scrubland to one side of the house. The engine cut out and the pilot ran towards her, bending low to avoid the still turning rotor blades. He took her bag, guiding her to one of the doors behind the cockpit.

Her father was sitting inside the helicopter. The shock almost made Arianna stumble backwards and he stretched out his hand, helping her into the empty seat next to him.

Arianna didn't object when he leaned forward to fasten her safety belt. If this was turning into National Surprise Arianna Day, then the world was making a fine job of it so far.

'What are you doing here?'

'In my own helicopter?' Her father shot her an innocent look.

'On Ilaria. You said you wouldn't set foot on Ilaria again.' Arianna frowned at him.

'Technically, I haven't…'

'You're going to rely on technicalities, are you?'

Her father smiled. 'Only you, Arianna. Everyone else allows me to talk them down, but you never did. Even when you were a child.'

Something about the fondness in his face reminded her of the way that Ben looked at Jonas. Warmth curled around her heart.

'I meant it. What I said the other day, about not wanting it to be another two years before we talked.' Saying it face to face seemed to cement Arianna's determination to repair whatever could be salvaged of her relationship with her father. To believe that some part of her relationship with Ben could be salvaged as well.

The lines on her father's face melted into a regretful smile. 'I made many mistakes, Arianna. I told myself that grief had pushed us apart, but it was my job to stop that from happening. I abandoned you and I would give anything for the opportunity to be there for you now.'

Arianna reached forward, taking her father's hand, realising that he was trembling.

'I need to go to England alone. But when I return I'd like to come to Athens, so we can talk. And I'd like you to come back here with me, so I can show you what I've done at the health centre.' Maybe that was a little too much to ask, but if miracles were possible then she might as well think big.

'I would like that. Very much...' The pilot had settled himself into his seat, and the helicopter's rotor blades began to quicken in readiness for take-off. Her father had to shout so that she could hear his final words.

'I'm so proud of you, Arianna.'

Arianna squeezed her father's hand. 'I'm glad you're here. Thank you…'

The helicopter swung out, across the darkening sea. The journey ahead of her, from the private airfield on the mainland to London, seemed very long and lonely. All she could do was hope that Ben would be there for her when she arrived.

CHAPTER FOURTEEN

MAYBE HE SHOULDN'T have sent the text. Ben had been considering the matter all night, before dragging himself wearily out of bed to take Jonas to the day-long play date for a friend's birthday. The other mothers there had taken one look at him and sent him home, telling him to come and pick Jonas up at six. He worked hard all week and he should take a day off.

In truth, a day off was the last thing that Ben wanted, because it gave him even more time to think. Had he worded the text right? Would Arianna understand that he wasn't expecting her to do anything about his great proposition, but that he just wanted to let her know where he stood? If she *did* know where he stood, what would she do about it? And if she rejected him, could he accept that decision, or would he just stubbornly keep loving her?

It was a lot more complex than just grabbing a couple of apple cakes. And the only thing that Ben knew for sure was that he'd never give up hope.

Now wasn't a day for hope, though. Whatever Arianna's reaction, he wouldn't be hearing from her just yet. If she deleted the text then he wouldn't be hearing from her at all, and if she replied she'd probably take a little time to consider what she wanted to say.

The weeds that had started to grow in the garden when he'd been away in Ilaria, and had continued untouched since then, were threatening to take over. He'd work for a while, until he was truly exhausted, and then take a siesta… No, he'd take a nap. Far fewer memories attached to a power nap than there were to a siesta, even if the two were largely similar.

He worked for an hour and then began to carry piles of weeds through to the front garden, tipping them into the garden waste wheelie bin. A limousine was travelling slowly past the house, and he wondered if someone in the street was getting married. If he'd been in Ilaria, then he'd have known exactly what everyone in the street was doing...

The limousine stopped and then backed up. Ben winced as it drew closer to a small blue run-around that belonged to his neighbour, and wondered whether going out into the road and waving his arms around to help the driver park was going to be necessary. But it seemed that not blocking the road wasn't his first priority, and he got out of the car and opened the back door.

Arianna got out of the car.

Wearing a pair of slim chinos, flat pumps and a striped T-shirt with a wraparound white jacket and standing next to the car, she looked somehow rich. She waved the driver back into his seat and banged impatiently on the front passenger window when he failed to draw away quickly enough, turning to smile and apologise to the driver in the car behind. Then she turned and saw him staring at her.

The car behind her shot forward, almost hitting her, and she jumped out of the way. Ben ran down to where she was standing, in between two parked cars, stopping before he got close enough to touch her.

'Not much of a rescue, if you're going to stand in the middle of the road.' He knew that he was smiling. Whatever she was here to do, whether it was to sink a dagger into his heart or take him into her arms and save him, he'd accept his fate because it would be at Arianna's hands.

'No. I could have planned that a lot better.' Her eyes were that mix of warmth and fire that made Ben hope against hope that she didn't have any daggers in her handbag.

'Come in.' Ben backed away from her so that she could step onto the pavement and kept his distance, leading her around to the back of the house. Arianna gave him a smile, picking her way around the weeds that were piled up on the path.

She stepped through the patio doors into the sitting room, looking around her. 'I like your house.'

Each one of the books in the bookcase, the toys collected up in a basket by the wide hearth and the chairs, a little faded with wear but still comfortable, took on a new lustre in Ben's eyes. If Arianna liked his house, then he liked it even more.

'I got your text.' She turned on him suddenly. 'So I came straightaway.'

'How...?' She didn't look like someone who'd been up all night, making her way through a busy airport and then spending five hours on a plane. She looked wonderful, like all of his dreams rolled into one.

'I called my father and asked for his help. He came to the island with a helicopter to pick me up, and then put me on his private jet to London.'

That was a story that Ben wanted to hear. Later...

'Do you need to call him to let him know you've arrived?'

She shook her head. 'No, he'll know that by now. The driver who brought me will be parked up around the corner, reporting back to him.'

Parked around the corner. Ice began to trickle into Ben's veins. Maybe Arianna wasn't planning on staying for more than a few minutes. She had a large leather bag over her shoulder that could contain a change of clothes, but on the other hand, it might be full of things to read on the plane home.

'Arianna. I'm sorry to drop this on you so suddenly. But I love you. Whatever you want to do with that is fine—'

She stepped forward, putting her finger over his lips.

'You made me feel that I'm worth your love, Ben. I want to accept that gift, and love you back.'

She'd changed. Maybe as much as he had. The Arianna who felt that she had no business being saved when her brother hadn't been was accepting his love. Ben almost fell to his knees as hope tugged violently at his heart.

'I meant it when I said I needed you to save me. I can't promise that I won't want to protect you, because I love you, but Jonas doesn't need a superhero and neither do you. I've hung up my cloak, and all I want is for you to love me...'

'I always have.' She smiled. 'So what do you think? You reckon that we *will* break each other, or that we'll be stronger together? I can't let you go a second time, and so you'll be stuck with me. We'll have to face whatever comes, together.'

'That sounds wonderful. You'll be stuck with me too.' He reached forward to touch her, and then realised his hands were covered in grime and his T-shirt had grass stains all over it. Wondering if he could break away for long enough to clean himself up a bit, so that he could feel the softness of her skin beneath his fingertips, was the most delicious of conflicts.

She saw his hesitation and smiled. 'I don't care how dirty you are, Ben. I really need a hug.'

He pulled her close and she melted into his arms. This was for real. It wouldn't break apart as easily as their previous embraces, and they both knew it. Ben kissed her tenderly, feeling the hunger in her kiss and letting it flow through him like a healing salve.

'Where's Jonas?'

'Play date. Back at six.'

'Oh. Good. I mean…not good, but…' Arianna kissed him again.

'I know what you mean. He'll be pleased to see you. Right now I'm *very* pleased to see you.'

She giggled, drawing back so that she could

tug his T-shirt over his head. 'I'm very pleased to see you too.' Her fingers moved to the waist-band of his jeans and Ben grinned, catching her hand.

'Not so fast.' He took her bag from her shoulder, putting it down on the sofa. 'I hope you've come prepared.'

'I'm prepared for anything, Ben. Every-thing.'

She ran her fingers across his chest and Ben felt each muscle quiver under her touch. This was a strength he hadn't known he had. He and Arianna, together. He slipped her jacket from her shoulders and then pulled her T-shirt over her head. Her skin was just as delicious as he remembered it.

'*Everything* is going to take a very long time, Arianna.'

'A lifetime?'

He kissed her. Any moment now he was going to carry her upstairs, strip her of her clothes, taking a suitable amount of time to admire the fancy underwear that he reckoned she had on, and then maybe they'd take a shower together, before they made the sweet-est love that he could imagine. But for now it was enough just to kiss her, feeling all the warmth of knowing that she loved him just as much as he loved her, and that they'd always be there to save each other.

'I'm not sure that one lifetime is going to be long enough.'

EPILOGUE

Two years later

THE CHRISTENING PARTY for Arianna and Ben's twin baby girls was in full swing. People had spilled out onto the beach, and a good number of them wouldn't be going home until the sun had set and then risen again.

Arianna nudged Ben. 'Are you seeing what I'm seeing?'

She pointed across to where the obligatory photographs were being taken, in the shade and relative quiet of the veranda. The two grandmothers had already posed, laughing and chatting together and insisting on swapping babies for even more photographs. Now her mother was cradling both babies and her father stood beside her, one hand resting on Jonas's shoulder and the other arm around his ex-wife, who was wearing a gorgeous red dress.

'Yeah. Your mother and father are looking pretty cosy these days. You think we need to put them under surveillance?'

Arianna smiled. 'Maybe. Perhaps Jonas can be our inside man and report back to us.'

Jonas would be staying with his beloved Pappous Ioannis and Yia-Yia Alexandra for two weeks at their villa in the mountains, along with Ben's parents. He was looking forward to being the centre of attention of four fond grandparents and it would give Arianna and Ben some time to spend together. After the hustle and bustle of preparing for two new babies, that would be welcome.

It hadn't always been easy, and never straightforward. Where to live, what was best for Jonas and where both Arianna and Ben could work effectively had been their first hurdle. Jonas's love of island life, and the English school on the mainland, where he could learn Greek and transition smoothly onto a Greek high school had been one deciding factor. The fact that there was a lot more left to do on the islands of Ilaria and Kantos, another. And their families got on so well that there was no question of Ben missing his parents or Jonas his grandparents, because they always had at least two invitations to stay for a while from Arianna's extended family. There was talk of them buying a place on Kantos when Ben's father retired, so that he and Arianna's father could spend their summers fishing together. Arianna's mother had confided in Ben that it was about time he slowed down a bit, and loosened his grip on his business empire.

They'd had their challenges. Ben had been required to study hard to get his Greek to a point where he could practise medicine on the islands. Arianna had experienced severe morning sickness at the start of her pregnancy, and as it had progressed the workload of the practice had fallen squarely on Ben's shoulders. Ben had clashed with Arianna's father over his plans for the large house on the island he was planning to build for them, insisting that the proceeds of the sale of his house in London made him perfectly capable of providing for his own family. Arianna had stubbornly refused to live anywhere else but her own house, and they'd come to a compromise that made everyone happy. The

L-shaped extension to Arianna's house was in the style of the rest of the house, and nestled amongst lemon and orange trees that Ben had planted. Arianna's father had gifted the shaded open-air swimming pool on the other side of the property for their wedding day.

Ben had taken over responsibility for the new health centre that was being built on Kantos, which would work in the same way as the one on Ilaria, servicing both the hotel and the village. Now, his morning commute was a walk down the beach to the boat moored at the small jetty they'd constructed, so that he could take Jonas to school before he went onto work.

'How did we ever get to be this lucky?' Arianna looked around at the group of friends and family, and the idyllic setting of their home.

'I guess…we didn't rely on luck. Whatever happened, we would have made things work.' Ben put his arm around her shoulders.

'So what do you put it down to, then?'

He thought for a moment. 'A lot of talking. Some arguing.'

'Make-up sex?' She stood on her toes, whispering in his ear.

'Yeah. I'm particularly fond of that. Watch out, I may have to pick a fight with you later.' Ben grinned down at her, then fished his phone out of his pocket, answering the call.

'Don't tell me... *Surely* no one's ill, are they? Isn't pretty much everyone here?'

'Mrs Panagos. Her nephew stopped by to pick her up and she's not feeling so good. He can't find her tablets.'

Arianna rolled her eyes. 'Well, if she went to the chemist and filled her prescriptions then she'd have them to hand when she needed it, wouldn't she?'

Ben nodded. 'Yeah, I'll have a word with her nephew and see if he can't pick them up for her. I'll be fifteen minutes, tops and I'll bring them back here with me, so we can keep an eye on her.'

'Okay. Good thought. I'll be making good use of my time while you're gone.'

'Interrogating your parents?' Ben knew how much her parents' new-found relationship meant to Arianna.

'Yes. If Jonas helps me out then fifteen

minutes should be more than enough to get the full story out of them…'

Ben skirted the house, slipping out through the olive trees that bounded the property. Something made him stop and look back, and he saw Arianna. He wouldn't have thought it possible to love her any more than yesterday, and then today had dawned. Who knew what tomorrow might bring?

* * * * *

LET'S TALK

Romance

For exclusive extracts, competitions and special offers, find us online:

- **f** facebook.com/millsandboon
- **⊙** @millsandboonuk
- **𝕏** @millsandboon

Or get in touch on 0844 844 1351*

For all the latest titles coming soon, visit millsandboon.co.uk/nextmonth

*Calls cost 7p per minute plus your phone company's price per minute access charge